Cursed with a poor sense of direction and a propensity to read, **Annie Claydon** spent much of her childhood lost in books. A degree in English Literature followed by a career in computing didn't lead directly to her perfect job—writing romance for Mills & Boon—but she has no regrets in taking the scenic route. She lives in London: a city where getting lost can be a joy.

WITHDRAWN

FROM DOCTOR
TO PRINCESS?

ANNIE CLAYDON

MILLS & BOON

Published in Great Britain 2018
by Mills & Boon, an imprint of HarperCollins*Publishers*
1 London Bridge Street, London, SE1 9GF

© 2018 Annie Claydon

ISBN: 978-0-263-93361-1

MIX
Paper from
responsible sources
FSC® C007454

This book is produced from independently certified FSC™ paper
to ensure responsible forest management.
For more information visit www.harpercollins.co.uk/green.

Printed and bound in Spain
by CPI, Barcelona

CHAPTER ONE

THE LEATHER CAR seat creaked slightly as Crown Prince Hugo DeLeon shifted, trying to find a more comfortable position. There wasn't one. He'd only been out of the hospital for twenty-four hours, and the pain in his left shoulder was normal. It would subside in a day or so, and he knew that impatience wasn't going to make him heal any faster.

All the same, he *was* impatient. And if his father thought that he was helping Hugo to get back to normal, then he wasn't.

There wasn't a great deal of choice in the matter, though. The King of Montarino was accustomed to being obeyed, and when he had visited his only son in the discreet private ward of the hospital, he'd made it clear that he was taking no arguments. He'd smiled at Hugo, in much the same way as any father would, and told him that his duty to his country was clear and very simple. He had to get better.

In order to make sure that his son's recovery went smoothly, the King had recruited a doctor who would stay with him at all times over the next month or so. Hugo had still been drowsy from the anaesthetic and his back hurt from having lain still while the pacemaker had been inserted into his chest, but he had got the message. His father didn't trust Hugo to look after himself, and so he was appointing a minder to do it.

He hadn't told Hugo much about this minder, other than

that she was a woman, eminently qualified, and that she was due to fly out from London today. The last detail was another smart move on his father's part, because Hugo knew most of the doctors in the small principality of Montarino, particularly those who were well qualified in cardiology. He might well have been able to wriggle out of the arrangement with any one of them, but this woman was an unknown quantity.

He wondered briefly whether she'd come equipped with tranquillisers and physical restraints. And, more to the point, whether she'd been briefed about the requirement for discretion. Hugo assumed that she had, because discretion was one of the codes that his family lived by, and his father never let anyone forget it.

'That'll be her...' His bodyguard sat in the front seat of the car, and had the advantage of an unobscured view. Hugo squinted through the tinted windows, and saw the chauffeur walking across the forecourt towards the airport's short-stay car park. Beside him was a young woman with mid-brown hair and a supple sway to her walk, which made the short hairs at the back of Hugo's neck prickle slightly.

Probably another one of his father's carefully reasoned choices. Hugo had to admit that he wasn't known for saying no to beautiful women, but unusually the King had misjudged the situation this time. A career woman, particularly a doctor, wasn't someone that he could contemplate giving any part of his heart to.

'She doesn't look too formidable.' Ted spoke in English, turning slightly in his seat to display the hint of a smile.

'I wouldn't bank on looks. She's managed to keep hold of her suitcase, and I imagine that Jean-Pierre did everything he could to wrestle it away from her.' Hugo turned the corners of his mouth down. The first thing his father's chauffeur would have done was to try to relieve their guest of her luggage and wheel her suitcase for her.

'I must be getting slow, I missed that.' Ted had done nothing of the sort; he just hadn't seen fit to mention it. In the five years that he'd been with Hugo, since his retirement from the British police force, the two men had learned to read each other's thoughts and trust what they saw. It had been Ted who had happened to mention that he'd heard that the doctor was being picked up from the airport this morning, and Hugo had made the expected decision to go with the car to greet her. Sizing her up before anyone else at the palace got the chance to speak with her couldn't be a bad thing.

Ted got out of the car, walking to the rear passenger door and opening it. For all the world as if he were according Hugo the respect his position required, rather than helping him with the weight of the door. Hugo climbed out of the car, ignoring the tingle of pain that reached from his chest down his left arm.

Now that she was closer, Dr Penelope Maitland didn't seem as formidable as her old-fashioned name might lead one to suppose. She was all curves and movement, looking almost girlish in a tan jacket over a cream summer dress, creased from travelling. Her light brown hair glinted in the sunshine, and bare, tanned legs gave her the fresh, outdoorsy look of someone going on holiday.

Maybe the gorgeous Dr Penelope was a rare mistake on his father's part. This woman looked as if she was more likely to spend her time here enjoying the pleasures of Montarino, not nagging him about his health. When her honey-coloured gaze met his, there was a spark of recognition and she smiled. A carefree kind of smile that sent tingles down his spine and allowed Hugo to believe that she didn't have it in her to make his life difficult.

Then she stopped in front of him, letting go of her suitcase long enough for Jean-Pierre to grab it and wheel it around to the boot of the car. 'I'm Dr Maitland. I'm told that I shouldn't curtsey.'

Her voice was like honey but her tone was like steel. Clearly Dr Penelope wasn't going to be quite as much of a walkover as her appearance suggested.

'Thank you. I'd prefer it if you didn't.' Hugo held out his right hand, glad that the pacemaker was on the left side of his chest, and didn't hamper the movement of his right arm. Her grip was as firm as her tone. 'Welcome to Montarino. I'm Hugo DeLeon.'

'Yes, I know.' She shot him a questioning look, and Hugo wondered whether she was going to rebuke him for coming to meet her. He mumbled the usual invitation to call him Hugo, wondering if he'd get to call her Penelope. The name seemed suddenly as if it would taste sweet on his lips.

'Please call me Nell…'

Hugo smiled his acquiescence. *Nell* sounded soft and sweet too, even if it was a little shorter.

'You must be tired from your journey. We should be going…' Hugo's discreet gesture to Jean-Pierre prompted him to get into the car.

She raised one eyebrow. 'Yes, we should be going. I'm surprised to see you out and about so soon.'

Her words had an edge to them. If anyone should be feeling tired she clearly expected that it should be him, and Hugo had to admit that he was surprised at the effort involved in making a simple car journey.

'I'm grateful for the fresh air.'

At the moment, the fresh air was making his head spin. Hugo stood back from the open door of the car and she hesitated and then got in, sliding quickly across the back seat before Hugo could even think about closing the car door and walking around to get in on the other side.

All the same, he welcomed the move. On this side, the seat belt wouldn't need to rest painfully on his left shoulder. Hugo got into the car, and Ted closed the door before he could reach for it.

'Have you been to Montarino before?' Hugo had years of practice with small talk.

'No.' Nell shook her head, regarding him thoughtfully.

'It's very small, only eight miles across, but very beautiful. We have one city, half a mountain and, although we have no coastline, there are some beautiful lakes.'

'That's nice. I'll have to come back sometime when I'm not working. I probably won't have much time to see them this time around.' Her mouth was set in a firm line, and Hugo's heart sank. Clearly there was no hope of deflecting the redoubtable Dr Penelope from her intended purpose.

Four days ago, Nell Maitland had ridden home on the night bus, after the farewell party that her colleagues at the hospital had thrown for her. It had been the ultimate failure, after months of trying to work things out with the cardiac unit's new head of the department, and save the job that she loved so much. And now...

She was riding in a chauffeur-driven car, sitting next to a prince. It was an object lesson in how dramatically things could change in so little time.

'I gather you have a strong tradition of attracting the best musicians.' She smiled in response to Hugo DeLeon's indication of the Montarino Opera House, and the car obligingly slowed to allow her a more detailed look.

'We like to think that we can hold our own with the rest of Europe when it comes to our appreciation of the arts. You *do* know a little about Montarino, then?'

Anyone could use the Internet. Although Nell had to admit that the photographs didn't do the grand building justice. Its sweeping, modern lines, rising from the tree-lined plaza that surrounded it, would have made it a land-mark in the greatest of cities.

'Only as much as I could read in the last couple of days. In between packing.' Nell wondered whether he'd mind that she hadn't even known where Montarino was before she'd taken this job. It had just been a name, teth-ered somewhere at the back of her mind, along with a lot of other places that she knew nothing about.

Hugo nodded, smiling. 'That's one of the best things about living here. Most people have few preconceptions, and so we have the chance to attempt to surprise our visi-tors.'

And it seemed that Hugo DeLeon was giving it his best shot. Nell had been told that he was a doctor as well as a prince, and that her advice would be a matter of reinforc-ing a message that he was already well aware of. In other words, he reckoned that the physical limits that applied to ordinary people weren't for the likes of a prince, and he needed to be kept in check.

Nell had no idea in which direction they were supposed to be going, but she was aware that the car seemed to be taking a circuitous route past a number of notable build-ings, all of which Hugo was intent on pointing out. If he thought that was going to deflect her from her purpose, he was wrong.

'I'm looking forward to seeing the palace.' She smiled brightly, wondering whether he'd take the hint.

'We're nearly there now.' Hugo raised his voice a little. 'Jean-Pierre…'

The driver nodded, turning smoothly onto a wide, straight boulevard and putting his foot on the gas. It seemed that everyone here responded to Hugo's every word, which was the first challenge attached to this new appointment.

The ambassador, who had interviewed her at the embassy in London, had said little but implied a lot. He'd got her medical qualifications and the fact that she spoke French tolerably well out of the way in the first five minutes. Then he'd turned the conversation around to her patient.

'Hugo DeLeon, Crown Prince of Montarino, can be...' The ambassador had paused slightly before coming to a conclusion about how to describe it. 'He can be self-willed.'

Nell had read *arrogant* into his words and had smiled politely. She had experience of dealing with all kinds of patients, and self-willed wasn't a problem. Neither was arrogant.

What the ambassador hadn't warned her about was his smile. It was polite, appropriate, and yet it seemed to hold real warmth. His high cheekbones lent a touch of class, and his shock of dark blonde hair, no doubt artfully arranged to make it appear slightly tousled, added a boyish note. Green eyes gave a hint that Hugo DeLeon was capable of some pretty serious mischief. Nell would have to watch out for those eyes.

But however handsome he was, however his smile made her stomach quiver, Nell had a job to do. Her fingers tightened on the strap of her handbag, which lay comfortingly across her knees. A man had gotten between her and her job before, and no one, not even this handsome prince, was going to do it again.

White knuckles. Hugo was used to looking for the little signs that told him what people were really thinking, and he'd noticed that Nell was clutching her handbag on her lap like some kind of defensive weapon. Despite the firm tone and the clear hints that he shouldn't have come to the airport, there was a chink in her armour. One that he may well need to find and exploit if it turned out that the restrictions she placed on him got in the way of his current plans.

They'd driven through the grounds of the palace and the car stopped at the ceremonial entrance to allow them to get out. She gave the high, pillared archways a glance and then turned to him as the car moved smoothly away.

'My luggage…'

'Jean-Pierre will arrange for it to be taken up to your apartment.' A sudden flare of panic had shown in Nell's eyes, and Hugo almost felt sorry for her. But keeping her a little off-balance, a little over-awed was exactly what he wanted.

'Right. Thank you.'

'Perhaps I can show you around.' The palace was big enough and grand enough to disorientate her even further.

'I think that's best left for some other time.' She was as sweet-smelling and soft as a summer's day, but there was no getting over the determination behind it all. 'This… apartment. I was told that it would be next door to yours.'

'Yes, it is.' If Hugo had had any say in the matter, he'd have put her on the other side of the building, but he hadn't. His father didn't often step into his life, but when he did, he did it thoroughly.

'With a connecting door?'

So someone had told her about that, too. Or maybe she'd asked. Hugo had rather hoped that he could just keep the connecting door closed and that it would never occur to anyone to open it.

'Yes, that's right. It's generally kept locked…' Finding the key was an easy enough matter on the rare occasions that he brought a girlfriend with him to stay at the palace for a few days, but he was sure he could just as easily lose it.

'I imagine someone has the key. Being a doctor yourself, you'll understand the need to have access to your patient.'

'And I'm sure *you'll* understand where your duties begin

and end.' Since the pleasantries didn't seem to be working all that well, it was obviously time to make things clear.

'The ambassador outlined them, yes.' She pressed her lips together and Hugo imagined that the British Ambassador had deployed all of the expected diplomacy in the matter. 'The King's letter of appointment, on the other hand, was a little less circumspect.'

Great. So his father had decided that he needed to weigh in on that as well. And even if the tiny quiver at the side of Nell's mouth told Hugo that she was feeling over-awed and nervous, her cool gaze indicated that she wasn't going to let that stop her from doing her job.

'Perhaps we should talk, over some tea.' Since deflection wasn't working, maybe negotiation would. The next step would be outright battle, and Hugo would prefer to avoid that.

'Yes. I think that would be a very good idea.'

CHAPTER TWO

HUGO HAD OPENED the door that concealed the lift, and when she'd seen the old-fashioned gates, she'd slipped in front of him, heaving them to one side. Part of him was grateful, but a greater part decreed that as a gentleman, and her host, he should have been quicker in insisting he open the gates himself. When he motioned her ahead of him into the lift, she hovered annoyingly next to the gates, giving him no opportunity to open them when they reached the third floor.

He showed her to her apartment, leaving her alone to freshen up. That would give him at least three quarters of an hour to rest before he had to submit to another onslaught from her.

Hugo sank gratefully into the chair in his private sitting room and closed his eyes. This morning he had woken feeling invigorated, and it had only been the pain in his shoulder that had reminded him he was unable to move mountains. Wide awake, his body feeling the immediate benefit of a heart that was now paced and doing its job properly, he'd jumped at the chance of getting out of the constriction of four walls, but it had worn him out. His own advice to pacemaker patients—that they might start to feel better almost immediately but must rest and get over the operation first—would be given with a lot more certainty in the future.

Fifteen minutes later, a quiet knock sounded on the main door to the apartment and he shouted to whoever it was to come in, keeping his eyes closed. If someone was here to make the tea or fuss over him, then he'd rather they waited until he was strong enough to smilingly refuse their help.

'How are you feeling?' Nell's voice made his eyes snap open.

'Fine. Thank you.' Hugo's eye's darted to the clock above the mantelpiece. Surely he hadn't been asleep...

Apparently not. She was pink-cheeked, as if she'd just got out of the shower, and Nell had changed out of her travelling clothes and into a slim pair of dark blue trousers with a white shirt, open at the neck and buttoned at the cuffs. She looked businesslike and entirely delicious.

He shifted, wishing that the ache in his left shoulder would go away, and Nell stepped forward. Without any warning at all, she caught up one of the cushions from the sofa and bent over him.

Her scent was... It was just soap. The soap that was placed in all the guest bathrooms at the palace. But Nell made it smell intoxicating. The brush of her hair, one soft curl against his cheek, almost paralysed him.

'Is that a little better?' She'd placed the cushion carefully under his left arm so that it supported his shoulder.

'Yes. A lot better, thank you.'

Nell nodded, looking around the room as if she'd mislaid something. 'Does your apartment have a kitchen? Or do you have to send out for tea?'

'The kitchen's through there.' The desire to stay where he was battled with a strong disinclination to have her make tea for him. Hugo shifted, ready for the effort of standing up, and she reached forward, her hand on his right shoulder.

'I didn't go to all the trouble of arranging cushions for

you to spoil it all by making the tea. Stay there.' Her voice
was kindly but firm. It occurred to Hugo that if he didn't
feel so tired he might have delighted in having Nell be kind
and firm with him all afternoon, and then he reminded
himself that business and pleasure was a very bad mix.

He heard her clattering around in the kitchen and closed
his eyes. Listening to Nell was almost as good as watching
her, because he could still see her in his mind's eye. That
was another thing that was going to have to stop.

Nell found a set of mugs in the kitchen cupboard. It was
a surprise, since she'd expected that a prince would drink
only out of bone china, but a good one. She'd been up very
early this morning and could definitely do with a decent-
sized cup of tea.

She looked in the cupboard for biscuits and found a
packet of chocolate digestives. Things were definitely
looking up. Next to them was a packet of painkillers,
wrapped around with a piece of paper with a typed chart,
each dose ticked off neatly. Hugo had taken this morning's
tablets but was past due for the lunchtime ones.

He was clearly overdoing things. And her letter of appointment had spelled out exactly what she was supposed
to do in response to that likely eventuality. She had to make
sure that he took the rest he needed.

She put the tea things on a tray and walked quietly into
the sitting room. Large and filled with light, the furniture
was stylish but comfortable, allowing the baroque fireplace
and the gilded mirror above it to take precedence. Hugo
seemed to be dozing, but when she put the tray down, moving a small side table next to his chair, he opened his eyes.

'This is…quite unnecessary.' He seemed quite devoted
to the idea that there was nothing wrong with him.

'And these?' She raised an eyebrow, putting a glass of

water and his tablets down next to him. 'Pain's generally the body's way of hinting that you should slow down a bit.'

'I thought I'd take them when I got back.' He seemed to be watching her every move as he downed the tablets in one, then took some sips of water. 'Please. Sit down. We really must talk.'

It was almost a relief. It seemed that Hugo wanted to make their relationship clear as much as she did, and it was a grey area that Nell was feeling increasingly uncomfortable with. She put his tea on the table next to him and sat down on the sofa, reaching for her cup.

'The first thing I need to say is that your job here is strictly confidential.' Nell took a breath to protest that she knew all about doctor-patient confidentiality and he silenced her with a flash of his green eyes. 'More so than usual. I don't want anyone to know what your role is here or that I'm your patient.'

Nell felt her heart beat a little faster. 'Is there a reason for that?'

'Yes, there is. A very good reason.'

'I'd like to know what that reason is, please.' She injected as much firmness into her voice as she could.

Hugo smiled suddenly. If he was unused to anyone questioning his decisions, it didn't seem to bother him all that much. 'I imagine you've done your homework and that you know I've been working very hard in the last few years to raise awareness about heart disease and promote early treatment.'

'I know that you're the patron of a charity that has done a lot of work in the field…' How much work Hugo had personally done hadn't been made clear in the article she'd read.

For a moment, it seemed that finally she'd managed to offend him. And then he smiled. 'I'm a doctor and it's my mission. You have a mission?'

'Yes. I suppose I do.'

'Then you'll understand the compelling nature of it. Weakness on my part can only undermine the message I'm trying to give.'

Nell swallowed hard, trying to clear the rapidly growing lump in her throat. 'Or…it might be seen as a strength. That you understand…'

'My job is to make things happen. And I'll freely admit that I'm a prime example of someone who hasn't followed the most basic advice and sought help at the first signs of any problem with my heart. Which is inexcusable, since I have a very clear understanding of what those signs are.'

So he couldn't allow himself this. In Hugo's mind, his illness gave him feet of clay. Nell might disagree, but it was his decision.

'What you choose to share about your own medical issues is entirely up to you. Of course, I'll say nothing.'

He nodded. 'Thank you. I see from your CV that you've taken an interest in the psychological aspects of recovery from heart disease.'

Something about his tone gave Nell the impression that this irritated him. 'Yes, that's right. I did a module on the psychology of recovery at medical school, and when I decided to specialise in cardiac medicine, it seemed very relevant. I co-authored a study on patients' post-operative experiences, in partnership with doctors from five other hospitals.'

'I'd be interested in reading it.' He turned the corners of his mouth down, and Nell felt her muscles in her stomach twist. Maybe he'd decided that questioning whether he needed a doctor wasn't enough, and that he'd take a leaf from her ex-boss's book and undermine her by questioning her professional ability.

She stared at him, wordlessly, and Hugo smiled suddenly. 'I'd be interested to know which category of patient I fall into.'

That charm again. That smile, which seemed calculated to make Nell's head spin and throw her off guard. 'Psychology isn't a matter of putting people into boxes, it's a way of understanding what's there. I'm sure you know that already.'

Perhaps she should mention that understanding exactly why Hugo was so desperate to pretend that there was nothing wrong with him would be a good start in getting him on the road to recovery. Or maybe she should wait until Hugo was ready to voice that idea for himself, even if scraping through the layers of charm and getting him to admit to anything seemed likely to be a long process.

'Yes, I do. And please forgive me if my welcome has fallen short of expectations. Your presence here wasn't my choice, it's my father who thinks I need a minder.'

Nell swallowed down the temptation to take the bait. 'I'm a doctor. If my duty of care to you, as my patient, makes me seem like a minder then…' She shrugged.

Hugo leaned forward, the cushion at his side slipping to the floor. 'Why don't you go ahead and say it? I can take it.'

If he thought that she couldn't look into his green eyes and say exactly what she meant, he was going to find out differently. Nell met his gaze and felt shivers run down her spine. Okay, so it was difficult to do. But not impossible.

'If you think that I'm here to be your minder, then that says a lot more about your approach to this than it does mine.'

'I suppose it does. But I want to make one thing clear. Duty to my father and professional courtesy to you require that I listen to your advice. But I have specific goals, in connection with a project at the hospital, that need to be met over the next six weeks. I won't allow anything to get in the way of that.'

'Even at the cost of your own health?'

'I can handle it.'

The battle lines had been drawn, and in the heat of his gaze it felt almost exhilarating. Then Nell came to her senses.

In the last three weeks, Hugo had faced a crisis. If that appeared to have had no effect on him, then maybe that just meant he was more adept at covering his emotions than most. He was hurting and unable to trust his own body any more, and if his reaction to that was stubborn failure to face facts, it was her job to get him to a place where he felt strong enough to admit how he felt.

His smouldering green eyes were suddenly too much for her to bear, and she looked away. 'Compromising on the way you get there doesn't necessarily mean you have to abandon your goals. Let me help you.'

He thought for a moment. 'What kind of compromise did you have in mind?'

Nell took a deep breath. This might be the first of many hurdles, but she'd made a start. 'I don't know yet. I'll need to examine you first and hear exactly what your commitments are. Then we can talk about it.'

'All right.' He smiled suddenly, as if he'd just remembered that he ought to do so. 'I'll make an effort to be a model patient.'

Somehow Nell doubted that. 'I appreciate the thought. But you've a long way to go before you qualify for the title of my most awkward patient.'

This time Hugo *really* smiled. 'Shame. I'll have to try harder.'

'Yes, you will.' Nell rose from her seat, picking the cushion up from the floor and putting it back in place, behind his shoulder. 'You can plan your strategy while I go and get my medical bag.'

Maybe his father knew him better than Hugo had

thought. His doctor at the hospital had been highly qualified, deferential, and had treated the whole thing as if it were an afternoon at a health spa. Nell was something different. Honest, no-nonsense and quite capable of cutting him down to size when he tried all the usual diversionary tactics.

Dr Penelope. He didn't dare call her that, she'd told him she preferred *Nell*. Which was charming in its own way but didn't seem to sum her up quite so well. Fierce, beautiful and unstoppable.

It was a little easier to think when she was out of the room. A little easier to remind himself of the flat in London, right at the top of a tenement block, where the lift sometimes worked and sometimes didn't.

A little pang of regret for times that had seemed altogether simpler. The sofa that had creaked slightly under the weight of two people too tired to move and yet happy to just be together. The awful green bedspread that Anna had chosen, and which hadn't matched the curtains but which Hugo had liked because she had. It had been the one time in Hugo's life when duty hadn't weighed heavy on his shoulders. All he'd needed to do was work hard at medical school and love the woman who shared his life.

He'd brought Anna back to Montarino, two newly minted doctors, full of so many possibilities and dreams. The ring on her finger had been replaced by something more befitting a princess, but Anna had always preferred the old one, which Hugo had saved for out of his allowance. It wasn't until she'd left that Hugo had stopped to think that maybe she had been unhappy at the palace.

And that had been his doing. Anna had trained to be a doctor, not a princess. She had fitted the bill well enough, but it hadn't been her mission in life. Hugo had been too intent on pursuing his own mission to see that until it had been too late and Anna had been packing her bags, a ticket back to London with her name on it lying on the bed.

'If you'd just looked, Hugo, you would have seen that this isn't enough for me. I have a career, too.'

There had been nothing that he could say because he had known in his heart that Anna was right. He'd let her go, and had watched from afar as she'd risen to the top of her chosen field, like a cork held underwater for too long and bouncing to the surface of a fast-flowing stream. One that had taken her away from him, and had never brought her back again.

Since then, Hugo had confined himself to women whose career aspirations were limited to being a princess. And if he hadn't found anyone who truly understood him yet, then one of these days his duty would outweigh the yearning for love and he'd marry regardless. It had never made its way to the top of his to-do list, though, and it could wait.

The sound of a chair being pushed across the carpet towards his broke his reverie. It seemed that the doctor was ready for him now.

'Would you unbutton your shirt for me, please?' Nell sat down opposite him, briskly reaching into a small nylon bag to retrieve a stethoscope.

Suddenly he felt slightly dizzy. At the hospital, he'd submitted to one examination after the other, distancing himself from the doctors and nurses who quietly did their jobs while he thought about something else. But Nell was different. She challenged him, demanding that he take notice of what was happening to him.

'My notes are...somewhere...' He looked around, trying to remember where he'd left the envelope.

'I have them. They were emailed through to me yesterday. I'd like to check on how you are now.'

Whether he'd managed to throw any spanners in the works. Her meaning shone clear in her light brown eyes, almost amber in the sunshine that streamed through the high windows.

He looked away from her gaze. Hugo had no qualms about his body, he knew that it was as good as the next man's and that he didn't have to think twice before he allowed anyone to see it. But things were different now. The new, unhealed scar felt like overwhelming evidence of his greatest weakness.

Nell sat motionless opposite him, clearly willing to wait him out if need be. He reached for the buttons of his shirt, his fingers suddenly clumsy.

Hugo was finding this hard. Nell pretended not to notice, twisting at the earpieces of her stethoscope as if she'd just found something wrong with them. The very fact that he seemed about to baulk at the idea of a simple examination told her that Hugo wasn't as confident about his recovery as he liked to make out.

That was okay. Nell would have been more comfortable if she could maintain a degree of professional detachment too, but that wasn't going to work. The main thing at the moment was to maintain their tenuous connection, because if that was lost then so was their way forward.

'What about official engagements?' She'd pretty much exhausted all the things that might be wrong with her stethoscope, and perhaps talking would put him at ease.

'My father's beaten you to it. He's taken care of all my official engagements for the next month. There are various members of the family stepping in.'

'I'll have to be quicker off the mark next time,' Nell commented lightly, trying not to notice that he was slipping his shirt off, revealing tanned skin and a mouth-wateringly impressive pair of shoulders. She concentrated on the dressing on Hugo's chest, peeling it back carefully.

'There's still the hospital project.' He shot her a grin

and Nell felt her hands shake slightly. Being this close to Hugo added a whole new catalogue of ways in which he made her feel uneasy. The scent of his skin. The way she wanted to touch him...

'What does that involve?' Nell did her best to forget about everything else and concentrate on the surgical incision on Hugo's chest.

'We're building a new wing at the hospital. It's going to be a specialist cardiac centre, with outpatient services, a family resource department and a unit for long-stay paediatric patients.'

'That sounds like a very worthwhile project.'

'Yes, it is. And there's no alternative but for me to be out there, raising money for it.'

'There's always an alternative...' Nell murmured the words, clipping the stethoscope into her ears and pressing the diaphragm to his chest.

'The work's already started and we've run into some unforeseen problems. There's an underground chamber that needs to be investigated and made safe. With men and equipment already on-site, every day of delay costs money, even without the cost of the new works. If we don't raise that money, we can't afford to complete the project.'

'And you're the only one who can do it?'

'No, but I have the contacts to raise what we need in the time frame we need it. We're looking for large donations.'

Nell frowned. There might be a grain of truth in Hugo's assertion that he was indispensable and couldn't take a break, although she still wasn't ruling out the possibility that pig-headedness and ego were also factors. 'I don't know much about these things but...couldn't your father help out with a loan?'

'I'm sure he would have made a donation, and I would have, too. But the Constitution of Montarino forbids it.'

'Really? You can't give money to charity?' Nell's eyebrows shot up.

'We can and we do, but it's very strictly regulated. The royal family is only allowed to donate five percent of the total cost of a public endeavour, and that ceiling has almost been reached already. You can blame my great-great-grandfather for that—he tried to buy up key parts of the country's infrastructure in an attempt to maintain his influence, and so the legislation was rushed through. For all the right reasons, in my opinion, but at the moment it's an inconvenience.'

'But it's okay if you *raise* the money?'

'Yes. History and politics always make things a great deal more complicated.'

As a doctor, this wasn't complicated at all. But Nell could feel herself being dragged into a world of blurred lines. Hugo's charm, the way her fingers tingled when she touched his skin. That was one line she couldn't cross.

'So you have to rest but you can't. We'll have to be creative…'

Hugo chuckled. 'I'm beginning to like the way you think.'

'Don't start liking it too much. If your health's at risk, I'm going to do everything I can to stop you.'

'Noted. Does that mean I can do everything I can to stop you from stopping me?'

'If that means you're going to get enough rest, and make sure you don't compromise your recovery, then feel free.' This war of words was fast becoming a little too intimate. A little too much like the delicious push and pull of meeting someone who could become a *very* good friend.

But it worked. Hugo nodded, his hand drifting to his chest. 'So what's the verdict, then?'

'Everything looks fine. You can see for yourself.'

He shook his head, and Nell realised that she hadn't

seen him look down at his chest once. 'I'll take your word for it. So…the day after tomorrow…'

'What's happening then?'

'It's a lunchtime fundraiser. I get to sit comfortably in the sun and make a two-minute speech. Actually, you could come along if you like.'

'There are spare tickets?'

'I'm your ticket.'

Nell gulped down the realisation that she'd be there as his plus-one. What mattered was that she'd be there, which meant that Hugo would have a doctor, and hopefully a restraining influence, on hand.

'Okay. Let's see how you are tomorrow and make the decision then.' Twenty-four hours and a night's sleep might just be enough time to get her head straight.

'Fair enough.' His green eyes seemed to see right through her. And it was worrying that when he turned his gaze onto her, his lips twitched into a smile.

CHAPTER THREE

NELL HAD SPENT as much of the afternoon as she could un-packing. Laying things into neat piles and hanging dresses in the large wardrobe. Smoothing the already immaculate covers of the great bed, which would have dominated a smaller room but here was simply in proportion. It had been an exercise in restoring order, pushing back the chaos that seemed to follow Hugo like the scent of expensive aftershave.

He seemed intent on playing the host, inviting her for dinner in his apartment. Over a beautifully cooked and presented meal, Hugo talked about the charity that seemed so close to his heart. How they'd raised awareness about heart disease and increased the number of people who had regular 'healthy heart' checks. How they wanted to move forward and provide a centre of excellence, which would cater to both inpatients and outpatients, for all the people of Montarino.

It was a dazzling vision. And yet here, at the centre of it all, was a man who felt the need to risk his own health.

She returned to her apartment tired but unable to sleep. A long bath didn't help, and neither did reading a book. Nell scarcely registered the words in front of her, because Hugo seemed to fill her mind, chasing everything else away. He'd said that he would be going straight to bed after she left, but when she went out into the darkness of the hallway she could still see a sliver of light escaping under the connecting door to his apartment.

She could hear Hugo's voice, distant and muffled behind the heavy door. Either he was talking to himself or there was someone there.

Someone there. There were pauses, as if he was waiting for an answer and as Nell pressed her ear to the door she thought she heard another voice, this one too low and quiet for her to be even sure whether it was a woman or a man.

Whoever it was, they shouldn't be there. It was midnight, and Hugo should be asleep by now. Nell's hand trembled as she took hold of the door handle. Walking into his apartment and telling him to go to bed might be one step too far.

But they'd had an agreement. He'd promised. And Nell had believed him. The feeling of empty disappointment in him spurred her on.

'Hugo…' She opened the door an inch, and heard the soft sound of classical music, coming from the room beyond. 'Are you still up?'

Silence. Then the door handle was pulled out of her grip as Hugo swung the door open, standing in the doorway and blocking her view of the sitting room.

'This isn't the time, Nell.' He spoke quietly, as if he didn't want the person behind him in the room to hear.

He obviously wanted some privacy and the thought struck Nell that his companion might be a woman. She felt her cheeks flush red. The last thing she wanted to do was come face-to-face with a girlfriend, who for some reason Hugo hadn't seen fit to mention.

'I'm…sorry, but we had a deal, Hugo.'

'I'm aware of that. Something came up.'

'That's not good enough…' Nell stopped herself from telling him that he should be in bed. In the circumstances, that might be a catalyst for even more exertion on his part. She felt her ears begin to burn at the thought.

'It's not what you're thinking, Nell.'

'Really? What do you think I'm thinking?' If she really was that transparent then things had just gone from very bad to much worse.

'What I'd be thinking. But on this occasion, we'd both be wrong.' He stood back from the doorway, allowing her to see into the room. Two seats were drawn up to a games table, which had been set up by the fireplace, and an elderly man sat in one of them. He wore immaculately pressed pyjamas and held himself erect in his seat. When he turned towards Nell, his milky blue eyes seemed not quite to focus on her.

'Jacob, we have a visitor. This is Nell.'

'A pleasure, miss.' The man spoke quietly, in heavily accented English. Despite his neat appearance, there was something vulnerable about him.

'It's a pleasure to meet you, Jacob.' Nell went to advance into the room, but Hugo stepped back into her path.

'Nell can't stay...' He threw the words over his shoulder, turning painfully to Nell and motioning to her to comply. She didn't move.

Hugo took a step forward, and she took a step back, instinctively avoiding touching him. He pulled the door half shut behind them.

'Jacob is...fragile.' He was whispering, but Nell could hear both urgency and fatigue in his voice.

'I can see that. But you need your sleep.' Whispering back seemed rather too conspiratorial for Nell's liking but having Jacob hear what was going on didn't seem like a good idea.

'I'll take him back to his apartment as soon as I can.'

'No, Hugo. You said we'd take things as they came and that you'd accept my help. Let's give that a trial run now, shall we?' Hugo hesitated and she glared at him. 'I'm not going to walk in there and order him out.'

Silently he walked back through the doorway, and Nell followed him. Jacob turned to Hugo, a fond smile on his face. 'Hugo, my boy... What's going on?'

'Nothing. It's all right, Jacob. I've asked Nell to join us.'

'Very good.' Jacob seemed to approve of the plan, gesturing towards the draughts, which lay on the chequerboard tabletop. 'You play, miss?'

'Not very well.' Nell smiled at him.

'Jacob taught me to play thirty years ago.' Hugo went to pull up a chair for Nell and thought better of it, allowing her to move it across to the table. 'I used to sneak downstairs when my parents were out in the evening, and we'd play draughts and drink hot chocolate.'

'Hot chocolate!' Jacob's eyes lit up suddenly, and he gestured towards the pot that lay on the coffee table, along with two gold-rimmed cups and saucers. 'I remember now. Would you like some, miss?'

Maybe that would bring the evening to a close. 'Thank you. I'll get another cup, shall I?'

Nell glanced at Hugo, and he nodded, resuming his seat opposite Jacob. His smile barely concealed his fatigue and he was moving as if he was in pain. The sooner they could end, this the better.

As Nell walked to the kitchen, she heard the two men talking quietly in French behind her.

'Who is she, Hugo?'

'She's a doctor, and her name's Nell.'

Hugo repeated the words, no hint in his tone that this wasn't the first time he'd told Jacob.

'A doctor? What does she want?' Jacob's voice took on an air of perplexed worry.

'She's here for me. Not you, my friend.' Hugo's tone was smooth, reassuring.

'Where's she going?'

'Just to get another cup. We're having hot chocolate.'

'Ah, yes. Hot chocolate and draughts…'

Jacob's memory had become fragmented by time. Some things were still clear in his mind, but he was groping in the dark, trying to make sense of others. It was common in patients who had dementia, and it was clear that Hugo was trying to reassure Jacob by re-creating the sights and sounds of things he did remember. The sound the counters made on the draughts board. The taste of hot chocolate. But that was all coming with a cost to him.

She fetched the cup and re-joined the two men, wondering whether Hugo knew that she'd heard and understood their conversation. Smiling, she poured the hot chocolate and sat down. Jacob moved one of his pieces and Hugo chuckled quietly.

'You have me…' He made the only move possible, and Jacob responded by taking four of his counters in one go.

'Another game?' The old man still seemed wide awake, and Nell wondered how long this was going to go on before he tired and they could take him back to wherever he'd come from.

Hugo nodded, and Nell shot him a frown. He couldn't do this all night, but it appeared that he was perfectly capable of trying if it kept Jacob happy.

'Will you teach me, please? I know how to play, but I don't know the tactics.'

'Of course, *mademoiselle*.' Perhaps Jacob had forgotten her name again, but he remembered how to play draughts, and that was the way that Nell could keep him occupied while Hugo rested.

Hugo stood, giving Nell his seat, and retreated to the sofa. As she and Jacob set out the pieces, ready to play, he seemed to be dozing.

At least Hugo was relaxing, now. As they played, Jacob

became animated, suggesting better moves to Nell, slipping from French into English and then back again, sometimes in the course of one sentence. Finally he began to tire.

'Hugo's tired. He's ready to go to bed now.' Nell nodded towards Hugo. If Jacob had known him since he was a boy, then he would also remember taking care of him, and some part of that relationship would still exist somewhere in his head.

'Is it time?' Jacob glanced around the room and then at his own attire. 'It must be. I'm wearing my pyjamas.'

That posed a second problem. Nell had no idea who Jacob was or where he'd come from. But Jacob turned, calling softly to Hugo.

'Wake up, lad. Time to go to bed.'

Instantly, Hugo's eyes were open and he roused himself. Jacob clearly came first, however tired he was. 'Let's go.'

Nell was perfect. Hugo had been prepared to exert his authority and order her out of his apartment, but she'd realised Jacob's situation very quickly and had played along. More than that, she'd taken charge, allowing Hugo to relax and get comfortable. Despite all his efforts to conceal it, he had to admit that he was very tired.

He led the way through the quiet corridors of the palace, Nell and Jacob arm in arm behind him. As he ushered them through one of the back doors and across the small courtyard towards the neat row of cottages used by palace employees, he wondered whether she'd be quite as gentle and understanding when Jacob was no longer within earshot.

It took Celeste a while to answer the door, and when she did so she was bleary-eyed, pulling on her dressing gown. Looking after Jacob was becoming a twenty-four-hour-a-day task for her, and she'd clearly been fast asleep when Hugo had texted her to say that Jacob was with him.

He waved away her apologies and said goodnight, hearing Nell's voice behind him echoing the sentiment.

The door closed and he turned to Nell, watching as the smile slipped from her face. That capable, no-nonsense expression didn't fail to send a tingle down his spine, even if he was far too tired to make the best of whatever conflict was brewing.

'So, Jacob wanders at night?' She walked next to him back across the courtyard.

'Yes. I'd appreciate it if you didn't say anything about it.'

He couldn't see the flash of her eyes in the darkness, but imagined it there. 'This place is full of secrets, isn't it? How long do you think you can cover this up?'

'I don't need very long. Before I went into hospital, I was talking to Celeste about getting a carer for him at night so that she could get some sleep. I contacted her after I was taken ill and she said that things were okay and she was managing on her own.' He turned the corners of his mouth down. Clearly things hadn't been okay, and Celeste had just not wanted him to worry.

'Celeste's his daughter?'

'Yes. Jacob came to work here at the palace when he was sixteen, it's the only home he knows. My father's always said that he and Celeste have a place here for as long as they want.'

'So why all the secrecy?' Nell frowned, clearly bothered by it.

'When he heard that Jacob had been wandering at night, my father went to see Celeste and mentioned to her that a nursing home might be the right place for Jacob, and offered to pay the bills. Celeste took that as a royal command…'

'But he was really just trying to help.' Nell gave Hugo's father the benefit of the doubt. Maybe Hugo should, too.

'I'm sure he was. But Celeste doesn't think it's the right thing for Jacob and neither do I. Like I said, this is his only home and he'd be even more disorientated than he is now in a new place.'

'Okay. Let me get this clear.' Nell stopped suddenly in the middle of the courtyard, and Hugo felt the hairs on the back of his neck stand up. They were in full view of the palace, and he didn't take anonymity for granted the way that Nell obviously did. He saw a light flip on, and then back off again. Probably nothing.

'Your father thinks that the best place for Jacob is a nursing home, and you think it's best for him to stay here.' Hugo dragged his attention back to what Nell was saying. 'So instead of talking to him about it, you're going to get a night carer in, see if that works and then tell your father about it.'

When she put it like that it didn't sound the best way of doing things. But then Nell didn't know his father. 'Yes. That's essentially it.'

She held up her hands in a gesture of resignation. 'Okay. You have an agency in mind, where you can get this carer?'

'Yes…' Hugo had wondered how he was going to break the news to her that tomorrow he'd be busy making those arrangements.

'Right. Give the details to me. I can do an assessment of Jacob and talk to Celeste about what she thinks is best in the morning, and we'll get things moving. If we can get someone in for tomorrow night, then Celeste can get some sleep and think better about her long-term options.'

Her tone brooked no argument, which was generally like a red rag to a bull where Hugo was concerned. But Nell was right. And although he'd only known Nell for a matter of hours, he trusted her. She'd take good care of his old friend.

'Thank you. I'd appreciate that.' He started to walk towards the back door of the palace, where they'd be out of sight of anyone who happened to be traversing one of the rear corridors.

'That, of course, is dependent on your not taking advantage of my being busy elsewhere to do something you shouldn't.' Nell caught up with him.

'Of course.' He opened the door for her and she walked through.

'I'd feel happier if you said it.'

He could see her face now, shining in the dim light of the corridor. A little humour mixed with the kind of determined compassion that he reckoned must make her a very good doctor.

'My mother's intending to cheer me up over lunch tomorrow. You can hand her the keys to the ball and chain if you want.' Nell raised her eyebrows and he sighed. 'If you'd be good enough to see Jacob in the morning, you have my word of honour that I'll rest.'

A stab of guilt accompanied the thought that he'd been a little hard on Nell. For the last two weeks, he'd gritted his teeth and submitted as gracefully as he could to the authority of his doctors and nurses and the limitations his own labouring heart had put on him. Yesterday morning, when he'd arrived back at the palace, he'd resolved to leave all that behind. He had to get back to normal as quickly as possible if he was to achieve the goals he'd set himself.

None of that had anything to do with Nell, though. She had a job to do, and when she smiled at him, everything else seemed to retreat back into obscurity.

'Thank you.' She gave him a *now we're getting somewhere* smile. Maybe they were.

CHAPTER FOUR

Hugo looked rested and relaxed. Like someone who had spent yesterday in his apartment doing nothing in particular while Nell assessed Jacob and made all the arrangements for a carer to come and help Celeste. Which was just as Nell wanted things to be.

But today was sure to bring new challenges. Hugo had wished her a good morning, and Nell had responded by picking up his car keys and giving him a lecture about staying within his limits. Ted, his bodyguard, had flashed her a quiet smile and got into the front passenger seat of Hugo's car, while she fiddled with the driver's seat, pulling it forward.

'Remember to drive on the left.' Hugo's quiet voice had sounded from the back of the car, and she'd ignored him, slipping off her high sandals and starting the car.

Ted directed her through the morning traffic to a large house, set back from the road and gleaming white in the sunshine. She'd followed the ushers' signals and parked the car between two others, which would have cost her the approximate value of her own flat had she been careless enough to scratch them.

'You look very nice.' Hugo bent towards her as they walked together to the circle of awnings laid out behind the house.

'Thank you.' On the basis that she couldn't compete

with anyone here, Nell had decided on a plain dress with no jewellery. That seemed to fit well enough with Hugo's approach, a grey suit with a white open-necked shirt. No signet rings, no diamond tie pins. He really didn't need that kind of thing, he was striking enough already, tall and tanned, with an easy manner that marked him out as someone who would always be acceptable in any social setting.

She was introduced to their hosts, and Hugo kissed the lady of the house on both cheeks. A drink appeared magically in her hand, and Hugo shook his head when he was offered one, obviously feeling that the juggling of drinks and handshakes would be too much for him to accomplish while taking care not to compromise his recent surgery.

'Prince Hugo!' A middle-aged woman marched up to him, and Hugo responded to her greeting with a hug. His face and body showed no signs of the pain that it would have caused him, but Nell knew that his left shoulder must be pulling at the movement. Then someone brushed against his left side, and this time he jumped imperceptibly.

This was no good. Nell carefully slipped in between Hugo and the people on his left side, curling her fingers around his left elbow. She knew exactly which angle his arm would be the most comfortable at, and she made a show of seeming to hang on to his arm, while making sure that it stayed immobile.

A nod, and a smile in her direction. And then, just for her, a mouthed *Thank you*.

'Nell's here from London. A friend of the family.'

The woman who was with him smiled. 'What do you do?'

'She's in between jobs.' Hugo had obviously decided to speak for her, in case she got their story wrong. 'Taking a well-earned holiday.'

'I'm particularly interested in the work of Hugo's charity.' Nell decided that taking Hugo's arm could be forgiven, under the circumstances. Acting like a glove puppet couldn't.

'Ah…' The woman nodded. 'Well, he's risen to the occasion yet again. Are you going to make a bid for him in the charity auction? So generous of His Highness to donate a trip with him on the royal yacht as one of the lots!'

Nell gave her brightest smile. 'He didn't tell me that there was going to be an auction after lunch until yesterday evening. It would be rude of me not to put in a bid for him.'

The woman laughed, and Hugo smiled graciously. Nell gritted her teeth.

A seemingly endless amount of small talk was cut short by their hostess, and everyone found their places at the tables. Champagne was served, and Nell leaned towards Hugo.

'What happens if the amount I have to bid for you goes over the limit you can donate to the project?' She hadn't thought that would be possible last night, but now she wasn't so sure.

'You over-estimate my desirability.'

'Not really. These women all look as if they can spend a large amount on just a whim.'

'I'm suitably crushed.' He put his hand to his heart, not looking even slightly crushed. 'Remember this was your idea.'

'Were there any other options?'

'There's always another option. But your solution was the best.'

'So you weren't looking forward to entertaining some lucky girl on the royal yacht for the weekend?'

'What makes you think it's going to be a woman? The trip on the yacht is the point of it all—a family with children would enjoy it, too.'

Right. Nell would bet a pound to a penny that there

wouldn't be any men bidding for this particular lot. But telling him that would only add to the chorus of appreciation that surrounded him, and Hugo already seemed to be under the misapprehension that he could get away with almost anything.

'What's Montarino doing with a royal yacht, anyway? It's completely landlocked.' Nell hadn't thought to ask last night.

'It's moored in France. Montarino has an ancient treaty that allows us safe harbour there. Unfortunately the treaty doesn't mention bills for the marina, so we have to pay those.'

'So you were intending a three-hour drive to the coast, in addition to swimming and sailing and…whatever else you do on a royal yacht? You do know that you're not supposed to be driving for six weeks.' Last night this plan had seemed a matter of pretending to pay a nominal amount to get Hugo out of a fix. Now the stakes were looking a lot higher.

'I won't be doing any of that, though, will I? Not if you win the bidding.'

The look that she gave him made the large hole that this afternoon was going to make in his bank balance seem more than worth it. Hugo could have changed his contribution to this afternoon's auction to something that demanded a little less activity on his part, but the programmes were all printed, and somehow the idea of having Nell stake her claim on him publicly had made him lose touch with the more sensible options.

Lunch was eaten, and a frisson of excitement ran around the tables when the auctioneer climbed up onto his podium. Nell's hand moved to her bidding card.

'You're sure there's no limit?' She smiled suddenly and

the sunlight playing on the ornamental fountains, on each side of the group of tables, dimmed in comparison.

'I trust you.'

'That might just be your first mistake…'

She was enjoying this. It occurred to Hugo that Nell might be about to teach him a lesson, and the idea didn't fill him with as much dismay as it should have done.

Premier tickets for a football match, courtesy of Montarino's one and only football team. Seats for a hotly anticipated rock concert. Some silver jewellery, from an up-and-coming new designer, who had cannily decided that it would do her no harm to have her work seen by the guests here today, was snapped up after a bidding war.

'That's a beautiful piece. It'll really suit her.' Nell was completely caught up in the proceedings, leaning over to murmur the words in his ear as she watched the winner talking excitedly to her husband.

'Would you like one? I can have another made…' The abstract curves of the silver necklace would actually suit Nell far better than they would Monique LaTour.

'Don't you dare!' She turned to him, a look of reprimand on her face. 'For what she's just paid, she deserves to have something unique.'

Hugo thought about telling her that Jacques LaTour was a multimillionaire and that Monique had enough jewellery to fill a wardrobe. But he doubted the information would make any difference to Nell, and anyway her attention was back on the auctioneer's podium now.

'Now, a special treat, ladies and gentlemen. Hosted by His Royal Highness Crown Prince Hugo DeLeon, a weekend trip on Montarino's royal yacht.' A gratifying buzz of excitement ran around the tables. Hugo smiled in acknowledgement, and then glanced at Nell. Her champagne flute was in her hand, and she'd just downed the whole glass in one.

* * *

Ted would have to drive back, or they could call for the chauffeur. Nell was sure that something could be arranged, and she needed something to calm her nerves. Bubbles hit the back of her throat and she almost choked.

This was it. She was about to spend an unknown sum of Hugo's money just to have his company for the weekend and ensure he didn't over-exert himself, something she was being paid to do anyway. The doctor's common room would have had a field day with that, but suddenly she couldn't have cared less. This felt like an adventure, one that might wipe away all the slights that had hurt her so over the last year.

As soon as the bidding started, three women held their cards up. The auctioneer managed to come to a decision over who had bid first, and as his finger moved briskly to and fro the price began to rocket upwards.

Nell saw Hugo's head turn towards her, and caught a glimpse of his worried expression. Then she held up her card, waving it to attract the auctioneer's attention.

'Two thousand from the lady on the right…' Nell felt slightly giddy at the idea that she was spending this much money.

There were many more rounds of determined bidding and one by one her rivals shook their heads. When the auctioneer rapped his hammer, an unexpected burst of exhilaration made Nell catch her breath. A few people looked round at her as Hugo leaned towards her, smiling.

'I thought for a moment you were going to let me down. Do I detect an element of risk-taking in your approach?'

Let him think that. If this was an exercise in each keeping the other off-balance, it couldn't do any harm. Nell gave him a smile and reached for her glass, which had been refilled at some point during the bidding. Clearly one of the attentive waiters had thought she might need it.

Hugo's lot was the highlight of the afternoon. There were a couple more, to round things off, and then the ring of a silver spoon against a crystal glass called for quiet as their hostess got to her feet. She thanked everyone for being there, and introduced Hugo.

He got to his feet, smiling, and Nell saw more than one person smile back. Taking a sheet of paper from his pocket, Hugo scanned it and then tore it in two.

'Ladies and gentlemen, I had a speech prepared, but I find that there's little more I can do to add to this afternoon.'

Nell took a sip of her champagne. This sounded pretty much par for the course. This afternoon was all about delighting in smoke and mirrors, not getting to grips with the serious issues.

'First, I'd like to thank Yvette, our hostess today...' He paused as a round of applause ran around the tables, and Yvette nodded a smiling acknowledgement. 'Second, I'd like to thank you all for your generosity.'

He paused. Five seconds' silence, which was enough to catch everyone's attention. Hugo's timing was impressive.

'You all deserve to know what that generosity means. Under your placemats, you'll find a leaflet...' He held up a glossy trifold, and Nell looked under her place mat and found one just like it. 'We're not in the business of bricks and mortar, or of reputation, although we're rightly proud of Montarino Hospital's record of excellence. We deal in people.'

Hugo's gaze dropped suddenly to the trifold in his hand. Almost against her own will, Nell opened her own copy of the leaflet, seeking out the photograph inside that he seemed to be studying. A little girl in a pink dress, cuddling a battered teddy bear. She was smiling, reaching for someone or something behind the camera.

'I'll let these photographs tell you how much your kindness means. Thank you, ladies and gentlemen.'

Hugo sat down abruptly, seeming to be almost overcome by emotion. Applause ran around the tables, followed by a buzz of conversation, which seemed to be centred around the leaflets in everyone's hands.

It was a great speech. Short and to the point, and tugging nicely at the heartstrings. Nell had noticed that he'd put the paper he'd torn in half safely back into his pocket. She wondered vaguely if there had ever been anything written on it.

It didn't matter. If Nell had seen the reality of heart disease, and knew that it wasn't all smiles and teddy bears, that wasn't what today was about. She'd lost count of the amount of money that had been raised, and it seemed the auction was just the tip of the iceberg.

A middle-aged man in a silk suit had approached their table, and Hugo had turned in his seat to talk to him. He pressed a folded cheque into Hugo's hand.

'Thank you, Henri. We'll use this well.'

The woman standing next to Henri spoke. 'Next time, I insist on being the hostess, Your Highness.'

Hugo hesitated. 'You're too kind, Justine. Think about it...'

'No, I don't need to think about it. I've thought about things for too long and it's about time I did something.'

'I'll have Nathalie contact you, then. She'll talk through all the options with you.'

'I think I have an idea that will be perfect.' Justine brushed off any other options with a wave of her hand.

Henri smiled suddenly. 'We must be going. It seems that my wife has a plan that needs my attention.'

'You shouldn't work so hard, Hugo...' Justine frowned suddenly at Hugo and caught Nell's eye, reverting to English. 'Take him away, my dear. He is neglecting his responsibilities to you.'

Nell smiled, not knowing quite what to say, and Hugo bade the couple goodbye. When he turned, his face was suddenly ashen and drawn. This was the first time that Nell had seen Hugo betray any weakness, and he was obviously tired.

Nell leaned towards him, speaking quietly. 'We're going. Now.' She injected as little room for argument into her tone as possible.

'I think you're right... Yvette will wrap things up.'

Nell glanced across at their hostess and saw that she too was accepting cheques, tucking them into a small designer clutch bag that lay on the table in front of her, which seemed to contain little else.

'I'll...go and make our excuses...' Maybe something would spring to mind on the way over to Yvette's table.

'That's all right. I said we might have to leave a little early.' Hugo reached for an auction programme, taking a pen from his pocket and scribbling something on it, then beckoning to one of the waiters. The note was carried to Yvette, who read it and smiled over at them.

Whatever he'd written, it seemed that their hostess was now happy to allow them to leave with as little fuss as possible. Nell bit back the thought that they should never have been here in the first place. Perhaps this would serve as a lesson to Hugo, and he'd respect his own limitations a little better from now on.

He swayed a little as he stood, wincing in pain. Nell hung on to his right arm, supporting him as well as she could and ignoring the glances and smiles from the people who crossed their path on the way back into the house. If they wanted to jump to the conclusion that there was something between her and Hugo, then let them. She imagined that she was just the latest in a very long list, which had the virtue of rendering her unremarkable.

Ted appeared out of nowhere, and Nell breathed a sigh of relief. 'Would you be able to bring the car round, please, Ted?'

'Yes, Doctor.' Ted flashed her a conspiratorial smile and hurried away.

Hugo almost stumbled at the bottom of the steps at the front of the house, and when she put her arm around him to steady him, Nell found herself almost in an embrace.

'I'm sorry.' He made to pull away, but Nell held him tight.

'That's all right. We'll just get home, shall we?' She could see his car now, moving towards them, Ted at the wheel.

He nodded, and she felt his arm curl around her shoulders. 'Yes. Thank you.'

CHAPTER FIVE

HUGO HADN'T QUITE been feeling fine, but he had at least been in charge of himself. And then suddenly he'd hit a wall. The one that he told his own patients about and re-assured them wouldn't be there for ever.

If Nell hadn't been there, he wasn't sure how he would have managed. But she had, and he'd felt her next to him, holding on tight as he'd walked what had seemed like a marathon to get to the car. Somehow, her scent had strengthened him and stopped him from just sitting down right where he was and not getting back up again.

Ted had helped him back up to his apartment and Nell had fussed around, taking off his shoes and jacket and loosening the collar of his shirt, then making him lie down on the bed. He'd protested and she'd ignored him, and then suddenly a wave of fatigue had pulled him into sleep.

When he woke, the room was in semi-darkness. He could make Nell out, sitting by the window, reading in the last rays of the sun.

'Do you want me to say it?' When he spoke, it felt as if his mouth was full of cotton wool.

She looked up from her book. 'You can if it makes you feel any better.'

It did. Hugo pulled the bedspread down from his chest, sitting up slowly. 'I overdid it today. I felt okay and I was sure I could manage it but…I couldn't.'

She smiled and suddenly overdoing things and proving Nell right didn't seem such a bad thing after all.

'You know, of course, that this happens. After the shock of being taken ill and then going through a surgical procedure.'

'Yes. Primitive instincts. We fight to survive, and then, when the danger's passed…'

She nodded quietly. 'And now you have to come to terms with it all.'

'What if I don't want to?' The words escaped Hugo's lips before he had a chance to stop them.

Nell shrugged. 'That's just too bad. You can command it to go away all you like, but it's not going to listen.'

Maybe. But if he couldn't rule his own feelings, then he could return the favour and not listen to them. Not let anyone know his weakness.

He swung his legs slowly from the bed. They seemed strong again. All he'd needed had been to sleep for a while.

'You're getting up?' Nell was looking around the room as if she was trying to figure something out.

'I feel much better now. What are you looking for?'

'Your wardrobe.'

'Through there.' Hugo nodded towards the door to one side of the bed, and Nell got to her feet. It seemed she'd decided to lay out a change of clothes for him. The idea that she might stay and help him into them didn't seem quite as deflating as it had when the nurses at the hospital had done it.

'Oh…' She'd opened the door and put her head inside the dressing room. 'Sure you have enough to wear here?'

'I go out a lot.' Hugo chuckled. 'Casual is on the left, at the end.'

She disappeared inside the dressing room, and Hugo heard her opening drawers and closing them again. Then

Nell reappeared, with a dark polo shirt and a pair of pale chinos over her arm. 'Will this do?'

'That's great, thanks.'

'Bathroom?'

'Through there.' Hugo indicated another door, staying put. He wondered how far Nell intended to go with this.

She disappeared into the bathroom and he heard the sound of water running. Then she popped her head around the doorway. 'I'll take a look at your chest and then leave you to it.'

Hugo heaved himself from the bed and walked into the bathroom. She'd moved the shower chair in front of the basin, and motioned him to sit down.

'How do you really feel?' She bent down, unbuttoning his shirt.

He wanted to say that he felt fine. Hugo *meant* to say that he felt fine, but in her quiet, fragrant presence he couldn't.

'As if I've been hit by a truck.'

Hugo closed his eyes, feeling her slip his shirt from his shoulders and carefully threading it off his left arm. Coming to terms with the piece of cutting-edge technology that was now implanted in his chest was the easy part. It was the thought that he was somehow flawed that he just couldn't shake.

More flawed. He hadn't been perfect to start with.

He felt her carefully remove the dressing over the surgical incision. It was hard not to shiver at the touch of Nell's cool fingers.

'It's looking good. A little bruising, still, but there's no infection and it's starting to heal. It's a nice job.'

Nice job. She'd said that before and he'd wanted to turn his back on her and tell her that he didn't need that doctor-to-doctor reassurance. If he'd still had a gaping wound on his chest, a scar that would never heal, it might reflect the way he felt a little better.

'Take a look.'

Hugo had purposely *not* removed the dressings to see what was underneath. But it seemed that parts of his body answered to her and not him, and his eyes flipped open. The first thing he saw was her face, composed in a reassuring smile, and even though he knew that smile was probably something she wore for all her patients it did its job. He smiled back.

'What do you think?' She stepped out of the way, and Hugo found his gaze on the mirror above the basin.

'It's...' Hugo tried for a shrug, and felt his left shoulder pull. 'You're right. It's a neat job.'

She nodded and turned to the basin, leaving him alone for a moment with his own reflection. Hugo didn't like the way it made him feel and he concentrated on watching Nell instead.

Her hands were gentle but capable as they dipped a flannel into the basin, twisting it to wring out the excess water. In his experience, that was only a short step away from tender. She laid the flannel over his shoulder, her entire concentration on what she was doing. It felt warm and comforting.

'That feels good. Thank you.'

She nodded, removing the flannel and dipping it back into the water. Wiping it across his skin, careful not to allow any drops of water near the wound. He'd seen this so many times before at the hospital, and had always felt that this was one thing that no amount of technology or learning could replace. When the nurses washed a patient, there was a tenderness about it that spoke of the kind of care that only human beings could give one another.

And now he felt it. The warm touch of water against his skin calmed Hugo, and the suspicion that everything would be all right floated into his consciousness, with all the reassurance of a forgotten friend.

She leaned towards him, rubbing the flannel across his back. Stopping to rinse and then repeat, her movements slow and thoughtful, like those of a craftsman plying his trade. Hugo closed his eyes, not ready to let go of this feeling just yet.

She finished with the flannel and gently patted his skin dry with a towel. Then he felt her fingers on the top of his left arm, gently massaging. He knew what Nell was doing. He wasn't supposed to lift his left arm above shoulder level for six weeks, and it was common to get a frozen shoulder during that time. It was just straightforward care, but it felt like so much more.

'Would you like help to shave?' He opened his eyes and saw that Nell was now opening one of the sterile dressings from the box that lay on top of the bathroom cabinet.

It had been a while since he'd let a woman shave him, and then it had been purely for pleasure. Anna had done it, but since then he hadn't let a woman get to know him that well. Hugo regarded the shaving cream on the shelf above the mirror and decided against it.

'Thanks, but I'll go with the designer stubble.'

Nell gave him a half smile. 'It suits you.'

It was the one thing she'd said that betrayed some kind of emotion locked behind the caring, and it sent tingles down Hugo's spine. Nell checked that the new dressing over his wound was firmly anchored, and then turned abruptly, leaving him alone in the bathroom.

If it worked, then it worked. Society lunches and bidding for a weekend in the presence of a prince wasn't a strategy that Nell had been called on to adopt before, and neither was washing a patient. But talking to someone, learning what made them tick and suggesting ways of coping was.

And if the sudden closeness with Hugo had left her wanting to just touch his skin, simply for the pleasure of feeling it under her fingertips, then that could be ignored in the face of a greater good. Her job here was not really to look after him in a medical sense but to get behind his suave, charming exterior, and find out what drove him so relentlessly that he was willing to risk his health for it.

Nell rang down to the palace kitchen, wondering if anyone was there at this time in the evening, and found that not only was the phone answered immediately but there was a choice of menu. She ordered a salad, on the basis that it was probably the least trouble to make.

Apart from raiding the fridge, of course. Nell had suspected that the top-of-the-range fridge in Hugo's kitchen was pretty much for show, and when she'd opened it, she'd found a selection of juices and other drinks. Nothing that involved any culinary activity other than pouring. She could have made him a milkshake, but that was about all, and a decent meal would help him recover.

The formal dining room in his apartment seemed a little too much like keeping up appearances, when that was exactly what she was trying to encourage Hugo not to do. A small table on a sheltered balcony was better, and she opened the French doors at the far end of the kitchen and arranged two chairs beside it. It would have made an excellent place to cook and enjoy food, and it was a pity that Hugo's gleaming kitchen didn't look as if it saw too many serious attempts at cooking. Nell wondered what he would say if she expressed the intention of baking a cake, and smiled to herself. Maybe she'd try it, just to see the look of bewilderment on his face.

Their meal arrived, and Nell directed the young man who carried a tray loaded with two plates and various sauces and condiments through to the balcony. He looked a little put out that she'd laid the table herself, and adjusted the position of the knives and forks carefully.

She called Hugo, and he appeared from the bedroom, looking relaxed and rested. When Nell had chosen his clothes, she been considering comfort, and hadn't spared a thought for how well they might fit or how her eye was drawn along the hard lines of his body. Chest. Left arm. It was permissible to allow her gaze to linger there, on the grounds that she was checking up on him. The strong curve of his shoulder, the golden skin of his arm, which dimpled over bone and muscle, were both visual pleasures that Nell could pretend not to have seen.

'Thank you. This is nice.' Hugo pulled one of the seats away from the table, waiting until Nell sat down before he took his own place. Even now, he couldn't quite let go and let her look after him.

'I just made a call down to the kitchen. Is someone always there?'

'No, not always. My parents are hosting a dinner party tonight.' He smiled at her, and in the muted lights that shone around the perimeter of the patio his face seemed stronger. More angular and far more determined, if that was even possible.

'So calling down for a midnight snack is usually out of the question.' Nell picked up her fork, stabbing at her food.

'Yes.' He grinned. 'If I want a midnight snack, I usually have to walk all the way down there and make it myself. Life at the palace can be unexpectedly hard at times.'

Nell couldn't help smiling in response to the quiet joke. Hugo knew exactly how lucky he was. Maybe not exactly, he probably hadn't ever battled his way around the supermarket on a Saturday morning, but he understood that he was privileged.

'If we'd been at my place, this might have been cornflakes. With chocolate milk if you were lucky.'

'You think I haven't done that?' Hugo looked slightly hurt. 'I trained as a doctor, too. You're not the only one who's eaten cornflakes with chocolate milk at three in the morning then fallen asleep on the sofa.'

Probably a nicely upholstered sofa, and not too much like the lumpy one that had been in Nell's shared digs, when she had been training. She wondered if Hugo's memories of medical school were quite as good as hers were.

'Where did you stay in London?' Holland Park, perhaps. Somewhere near the embassy.

'Shepherd's Bush. We had a flat over a pizza place for a while, and it always smelled of cooked cheese. Then we moved to Tottenham. That was a great flat, in a high-rise. You could see right across London.'

Perhaps his experience had been a little more like Nell's than she'd thought. 'It must have been a bit of a culture shock for you.'

He laid down his fork. 'People are people. That's what every doctor learns, isn't it?' He said the words as if he was explaining a simple concept that Nell had somehow failed to understand.

'Yes, of course. But some people find things easier than others.' Waiting lists. Doctors who had enough time to see to the physical needs of their patients but not always the opportunity to talk for as long as was needed... The list could go on.

'You met Justine and Henri earlier today. What did you think, that they were a couple of privileged people who like a nice lunch?'

'They...' Yes, that was exactly what Nell had thought. 'They were very generous.'

'Yes, they always are. They lost their son to heart disease when he was only two years old. Justine became very depressed and it was years before she would even talk about him. Holding a lunch event is a massive step for her.

It's not all about the money. Yvette lost her father to heart disease when she was fifteen.'

Nell felt herself flush. 'I'm sorry. I did think less of what they were doing because they're rich, and that was wrong of me.'

Hugo shook his head. 'You're not entirely wrong. A lot of the people who were at the lunch today were there because they wanted to be seen in the right places. But many of them have a real and personal commitment to what we're trying to do.'

'The little girl in the leaflet. She's really a heart patient?' Nell had had her doubts, wondering if the leaflet was principally an exercise in PR. It was important now, to know whether she'd been wrong.

'Yes, she is. One of my patients, in fact. She had her ninth operation a few days ago. She wanted to help me build her new clinic.'

Nell laughed. '*Her* new clinic.'

'Yes, it's hers. She might let a few other patients in if she likes them. No boys. And she wants it to be completely pink, like a giant marshmallow.' He was smiling now.

'Sounds like my kind of hospital.'

'So what *are* you doing here?' He asked the question quietly. 'You don't strike me as the kind of person whose ambitions lie in the direction of keeping errant princes in check.'

Hugo had a way of dropping the charm and cutting right to the chase. It was uncomfortable. 'I'm…in between jobs at the moment.'

'I saw your curriculum vitae. Someone with your talents isn't usually in between jobs unless she wants to be.'

He'd seen what the employment agency hadn't, and there was no explaining it away with clichés. Nell wanted to tell him the whole truth, but that probably wouldn't be all that wise.

'My last job was challenging, both professionally and personally. I want to spend six months looking around for another that will...'

'Just be challenging professionally?'

Nell caught her breath. How did he know so much about human nature, when he seemed so protected from it? 'Something like that.'

'So you thought that one patient might be a bit of a holiday.' He was taking her apart, piece by piece, and Nell felt powerless to stop him. 'But I imagine you're someone who gets a little bored on holiday.'

She could feel her cheeks heating up. She wasn't going to give Hugo the satisfaction of admitting that he was absolutely right. He held her gaze for a moment longer, and then leaned slowly back in his chair. Maybe he'd already seen what he wanted to see, and her reply was unnecessary.

'Then maybe I should consider diversionary tactics. To keep you from feeling that you're wasting your time here.'

He reached for the bottle of water on the table, and Nell took it from him. 'How can I be wasting my time when there are bottles to be opened?'

If he could hide his innermost feelings under a layer of charm, then so could she.

CHAPTER SIX

THE SUMMONS HAD arrived first thing the following morning, and Nell had followed the messenger to the King's study. Despite the early hour, he was already working at his desk. He had offered her a cup of coffee and then pushed the morning paper towards her.

The King hadn't expressed the horror that Nell had felt when she'd looked at the pictures on the front page. It was just one of those things, an innocent action could be misinterpreted under the glare of scrutiny that the royal family were subjected to. But he had taken issue with a number of other things.

Nell had felt her heart close. Unable to look at him, she'd given no reason as to why she and Hugo had been seen at the back entrance to the palace at one in the morning. How could she? She'd promised to keep silent about the business with Jacob and Celeste until Hugo had had a chance to approach his father.

The King moved on to why exactly she'd been seen bidding for Hugo's company at the auction yesterday. This time Nell did have an answer, even if it wasn't a very good one.

'It was my idea. I thought that…well, it's too much for him to be hosting a weekend like that so soon after the operation. And Hugo wouldn't back out.'

'And you didn't consider how it might look?' The King's

tone wasn't unkind, but it was very firm. He tapped the paper with one finger. 'My real concern though, is that it's clear to me that this photograph does not show an embrace, as the papers seem to believe, it shows Hugo leaning on you. Your one responsibility was to ensure that he didn't take on too much, and damage his health.'

Nell nodded her assent, her hands clasped tightly in her lap. How could she object to the King's request that she submit a written account of Hugo's activities and medical condition every day, when she had already failed so spectacularly? And how could she complain when he hinted that unless things changed, he would be finding another doctor for Hugo.

She was trembling by the time the King dismissed her. Hurrying back to her apartment, Nell blinked back the tears. They were her own business, fit only to be seen by the four walls of her sumptuous bedroom.

Nell sat down on the bed, gulping for breath. She was just being stupid. The King had every right to ask questions, and if he'd been unfair, it was because he didn't know about Jacob's visit to Hugo's apartment, and Nell hadn't enlightened him. This *wasn't* a re-run of all that had happened in her last job.

All the same, it had a similar sting to it. Nell had rejected Martin's advances, and he'd taken advantage of his position as her boss to deliver payback. She'd come to dread seeing him on the ward, because there had always been some barb or put-down. And she'd learned to sit in silence when he'd called her to his office, because replying to his catalogue of her faults and flaws had only made things worse. She'd thought his anger might subside over time, but if there was one thing that Martin knew how to do, it was hang on to a grudge.

This wasn't the same. In some ways it was worse, though. The King had been painstakingly correct, and in his own way he'd been almost kind, but his concerns were justified. She couldn't put his criticism down to spite, the way she'd been able to with Martin. And she'd hardly looked back when she'd left the hospital, but leaving Hugo…already he was quite a different proposition.

There was nothing else for it. She had to get the crying over and done with, pull herself together, and do better.

She was expecting the knock on the connecting door between their apartments. Hugo would have finished his breakfast, and would be ready for another battle of wills over whether he was well enough to do whatever he pleased. Nell had dried her tears and was ready for him.

She opened the door, trying not to look at him, just in case he happened to be smiling. Hugo's smile was his most effective weapon.

'You did too much yesterday. You need to rest today.'

He raised one eyebrow. 'All right. Now that you've got that off your chest, would you like to join me for coffee?'

Maybe she could have waited a little longer than two seconds to say it. 'Yes. Thank you.'

'You've had breakfast?' He moved away from the door, leaving Nell to follow him into his sitting room.

'No, I…' Saying that she felt sick with apprehension wasn't the best way of appearing strong. 'Coffee's fine.'

'Right.' The tray was standing ready on the table, and he filled two cups, watching silently as Nell added milk to hers. 'What's the matter?'

'Nothing.' She smiled breezily at him, and he frowned.

'So I'm going to have to make a guess, am I?'

Nell puffed out a breath. Maybe she should tell him, he'd probably hear about it anyway. And perhaps Hugo would respect his father's wishes better than he did her advice.

'The King called me to see him this morning. He's not happy.'

'He isn't happy about a lot of things. Ignore him.'

'I can't ignore him. Apart from the fact that he happens to be the King, he's also my employer.'

'I'm Crown Prince, don't I get a say?' Hugo grinned, and Nell ignored the temptation to forgive him anything and everything.

'This isn't a game, Hugo. If you want to bait your father then go right ahead and do it, but don't put your own health at risk just because you won't admit that he's right.' Nell pressed her lips together. She could have put that more tactfully, but right now she wasn't in the mood to do so.

He was suddenly solemn, his gaze searching her face. Nell felt herself redden, the tears that she'd only just managed to control pricking at the corners of her eyes.

'What did my father say to you?'

'He heard about you being up so late the other night. There was nothing I could say to him in response, without telling him about Jacob.'

'So you took the blame yourself.' His frown grew deeper.

'What else could I do? He heard about my bidding at the auction as well. And there are photographs of me supporting you to the car in this morning's papers.'

'He can't hold you responsible for that.' Hugo pressed his lips together, obviously aware of the conclusion that the papers had drawn.

'He doesn't. But he holds me responsible for the fact that you're doing too much. He says that things have to change and that from now on I have to submit a daily report to him.'

'Nell, I'm sorry. I'll make it right.' His jaw hardened into a determined line.

'No, you won't. You can't. But if you're reckoning on carrying on like this, then tell me now, because I'd rather leave than be fired.'

'No one's going to fire you, Nell.'

She shook her head silently. Hugo didn't understand, he'd never been squeezed out of a job or bullied by a boss. He was the golden boy, who everyone wanted.

Even Nell wanted him. Despite all her exasperation, she'd started to enjoy their battles, almost to look forward to them. And in doing so, she'd forgotten the reason why she was here.

'There's a meeting arranged for this afternoon at my charity's offices. It's only going to be for an hour, the construction company is going to update us on how things are going. If I asked everyone to come here instead, I'd find it less taxing.'

Hugo's tone was almost contrite. When Nell looked up at him, there was a trace of concern on his face.

This was a start. 'That sounds like a good idea, Hugo.'

Shame was something that Hugo usually tried to avoid. If he worked hard, and met the standards that he set, he generally found that he could live with himself. But now he felt thoroughly ashamed.

Being ill had made him crazy. It had stripped away the feeling that he was in charge of his life, and he was struggling to find the man he'd once thought himself to be. But in trying to pretend that it hadn't happened, he'd hurt Nell, and that was unforgiveable.

He knew exactly where his parents would be during the week, they were creatures of habit. As he expected, he found them sitting at the twin desks, placed back to back to allow murmured conversation and smiles while they completed their correspondence for the day.

'Mother...' He smiled, and his mother rose for a hug, made awkward by his lame shoulder.

'Hugo, darling. How do you feel today?'

'Much better, thank you.' Hugo's relationship with his

mother was an effortless synergy of respect for her position and warmth. The one with his father involved rather more effort. 'I'd like to speak with Father.'

His mother sat firmly back down, waving her hand towards his father, who had looked up from the papers in front of him. Her smile told Hugo that she knew exactly what all this was about, and she wasn't going to give either of them the chance to argue in private.

'Go ahead, darling. He's right here, in case you didn't notice.'

Right. Hugo turned to his father, and found himself locked in the familiar combative stare that was their usual greeting to each other. He sat down, knowing that it probably wouldn't defuse the situation. Pacing up and down wasn't going to help much if he wanted to imply that he was taking things easy.

'It's not Nell's fault, Father.'

His father turned the corners of his mouth down. 'I'm inclined to agree with you. It is, however, Dr Maitland's responsibility to make sure that you rest.'

'And she's doing that.'

'I disagree, Hugo.'

The silence between them wasn't broken by his mother's voice. Usually her intervention avoided conflict between father and son, neatly suggesting a solution that everyone could live with. But this time there was just a silence.

'My behaviour isn't her fault. Nell's a good doctor, and…she's exactly what I need at the moment. In the future, I'll follow her instructions.' This was a climb-down of gargantuan proportions. But Hugo had seen humiliation and rejection in Nell's face this morning, and they haunted him.

'So things are going to change, are they?'

'They will. Don't punish her in order to get to me.'

His father leaned back in his chair. 'You've seen the papers this morning?'

'It'll blow over. How many other young women have been photographed in my company in the last year?'

'Goodness only knows. I don't know where you get the time,' his mother interjected suddenly, and both men turned on her, frowning. 'It's just an observation, darling. It would make things a great deal easier if you decided that your health wasn't such a secret.'

'I want it to remain private.'

That was one of the few things that Hugo and his father had agreed on lately, even if it was for different reasons. His father had always drawn a line between his family's personal lives and their public duties, and that had allowed Hugo to grow up outside the glare of publicity. For Hugo, it was more a matter of not wanting to be seen as irrevocably flawed.

King Ferdinand nodded. 'You know I have no argument with you there, Hugo. But you have a duty…'

Hugo nodded impatiently. 'I know what my duty is. To be strong enough to serve the people.'

His father nodded. 'I assume from your presence that Dr Maitland *wants* to stay.'

'I have no idea. But *she* gets that choice.' Hugo felt his heart quicken and he ignored it. He would have to stop gauging everything by the beat of his own heart.

'There's only one person who can make sure that Dr Maitland keeps her job. That's you, Hugo.'

Hugo got to his feet, making an effort to swallow his anger as he turned to his mother. He bade her goodbye, omitting the same gesture towards his father, before turning and walking out of the room.

Hugo had been oddly compliant all day. It was as if he'd suddenly come to his senses, or at least decided that it was more politic to appear to have done so. He'd spent the morning reading through the reports from the construction company, and the meeting was a short one. Nell had been able to relax a little and take an interest in the plans for the clinic. She could see why the project excited Hugo, and why he was willing to give up almost anything to see it come to fruition.

'What did Celeste say?' Nell had gone to speak to Celeste alone, while he stayed in his apartment.

'She said that last night, when the carer was with them, she got the first good night's sleep she's had in months.'

Hugo nodded. 'That's something. It's working, then?'

'It's early days. But, yes, I think it'll work very well.'

'Good. I'll speak to my father…'

'Not yet, Hugo. I… I've already taken the blame for the other night, and I'm still in one piece. Let's wait a week and make sure that the arrangement's working for Celeste first. Then you can speak to him.'

'He should know now. That you weren't to blame for that either.'

Either? 'You've already spoken to him, haven't you?'

'Yes. I told him that yesterday was entirely my fault and that it wouldn't happen again.'

The sudden feeling of warmth in Nell's chest caught her by surprise. Nell didn't dare wonder if she was really that important to Hugo, that he'd comply with his father's wishes for her sake.

'You didn't need to do that… But thank you.'

'My pleasure. There are always plenty of other options when it comes to defying my father. You'd be surprised at the scope his position affords.'

He was making light of it, but the look in his eyes said something different. That she could trust him and he'd be there for her.

The sound of the bell, at the front door of the apartment

broke the silence. It couldn't have come at a more inopportune time, and Nell willed him to ignore it, but he didn't, rising from his seat. Maybe he was glad of the interruption.

She heard voices in the hallway, and jumped to her feet when Queen Margaux entered the room. She was more casually dressed than in the pictures Nell had seen on the Internet, wearing a pair of tan trousers and a matching shirt, but she was still immaculate.

'I'm glad to see that you're here, resting, Hugo.' Queen Margaux bestowed a smile on Nell that seemed to indicate she thought Nell had something to do with that. 'Penelope. I'm very glad to meet you.'

'She prefers Nell, Mother. Nell, meet my mother.'

Nell wondered whether she should curtsey, and remembered she didn't know how. Queen Margaux held her hand out and gave Nell's a surprisingly firm shake.

'I'm very glad to meet you, Your Majesty.' Nell hoped that was something close to the right form of address.

'Margaux, please.' The Queen dropped a slim file that she was carrying onto the table and sat down.

'Would you like some tea…?' Hugo's mother was obviously here to speak to him, and it was a good means of escape. It might be rude not to address the Queen by name, as she'd instructed, but Nell couldn't quite bring herself to call her Margaux.

'Thank you, but no. I've come to speak with both you and Hugo.'

'What about? If you're here to try and talk some sense into me, Nell already has that covered.'

Margaux flashed another smile at Nell. 'Then I won't go to the trouble. Anyway, this is far more pressing. I think you should both read this.'

She slipped two sheets of paper from the folder, holding them out. Hugo took them both and started to read.

'What is it?' Nell reached across, and he threw the papers down on the coffee table.

'It's rubbish. Outrageous… You don't need to see it.'

'If it's rubbish then it can't do any harm to look.' She picked up one of the sheets.

'You have to understand, Nell, that the papers will pay for stories, and people will make things up. It gives them a misplaced sense of importance.'

'All right. Let me read it, will you?' How bad could it be? Nell turned her attention to the paper and started to read. She immediately recognised the name involved. Three sentences in, she realised that it was worse than she could have possibly imagined.

'This is a request for comment.' Queen Margaux's voice broke through her horror. 'It's from one of the more responsible papers, and if I speak to the editor I can refute the claims and at least delay publication. If they can't get any corroboration then it'll stop it completely. But if the man making these claims goes somewhere else, that might not be so easy.'

'Is…there any indication he might?' Nell felt her cheeks redden at the thought.

'I had my secretary examine his social media pages, and it seems he's already shared the story that was in the paper this morning and made a few comments. Nothing of any substance, they're more of the *I know something you don't* variety, but it shows an intention. But you know this man, Nell, he's your ex-boss. What do you think?'

'I don't think he's going to give up.' Nell shook her head miserably. The one thing that neither Hugo nor Queen Margaux had asked yet was whether the allegations were true. It didn't appear that Hugo was going to, and his mother was clearly taking his lead.

She took a deep breath. 'I want to say…that it's not true. I didn't make any passes at my former boss, he was the one who propositioned me. And I'd never offer sexual favours in return for covering up my mistakes. The previous Head of Department knew me well, I worked for him for three years, ask him—'

'Don't, Nell.' Hugo interrupted her. 'You shouldn't have to defend yourself.'

'I want to. It's the truth.'

Queen Margaux turned to Nell, laying her hand on hers. 'I didn't doubt it, Nell. But thank you for clarifying things. This is a situation where we must be clear and direct in all of our dealings.'

'Yes, we can be clear and direct in completely refuting these allegations.' Hugo's brow was still dark.

'Of course, Hugo. But if you'd read the whole piece, you'd see that there's a reference at the end to a romantic entanglement between the two of *you*. If Nell's real relationship with you were known, then it might well defuse the situation.'

Nell shook her head. 'I'm sorry but…no. I'm Hugo's doctor, and it's my responsibility to make sure that if he wants to keep the details of his medical condition private, that's what happens. I can't allow it.'

'Nell, that's up to me.'

If Hugo was about to make an abrupt about-turn on the question of his own privacy, Nell wasn't. 'You've already expressed your wishes, Hugo, and while I don't altogether agree with them, it's my duty to uphold them. I won't have it.'

'But—'

'There's always the Royal Agreement,' Queen Margaux cut her son short.

'That doesn't apply here, Mother.'

'It might. Since the papers seem already to be jumping to conclusions…' Queen Margaux reached for the folder, taking off her reading glasses. 'I'll leave you both to consider the options. But in the meantime, Nell, I want you to understand that you have my full support in this. We will do whatever it takes.'

Nell stammered her thanks, and Hugo rose to see his mother out. While they were gone, Nell concentrated on keeping breathing. Because it appeared that was about the only thing that Martin could never take away from her.

CHAPTER SEVEN

'I HAVE TO EXPLAIN.' Hugo had returned to the sitting room and was regarding her silently.

'No, you don't. I don't make a habit of explaining what the papers say about me...' He broke off, seeing the tears that ran down Nell's cheeks.

'I do...really.'

Hugo came to sit next to her on the sofa. 'If you *want* to tell me something about this, then I'll listen. All you *need* to say is that you want this stopped.'

'It's good of you to say that. I want to tell you.'

'Okay.' He was sitting close, but still not touching her. The temptation to ask for Hugo's comfort was almost too much to bear, but Nell couldn't do that. Not until he knew all the facts, and he believed her.

'When I was a student, Martin was a visiting lecturer. He was brilliant, he has a very fine mind.'

'Okay. I'll take your word for that.' Hugo didn't look very convinced.

'I went to speak to him after the lecture and he asked me for coffee. One thing led to another...' She glanced at Hugo and he nodded. 'I was dazzled. He was older than me, of course, and very handsome. He knew about loads of things that I didn't. Introduced me to a lot of new experiences.'

She expected Hugo to nod and understand. Instead,

he rolled his eyes. 'I've seen that type. No feeling of self-worth, so he has to pick on someone in a subordinate position to impress.'

His words chipped away at the dream. The feeling that Martin had been all-knowing and that it was she who'd done the wrong thing. She *had* done the wrong thing, and maybe Hugo would think a little differently when she told him.

'He was based in Newcastle, and he came down to London every couple of weeks. I saw him then and I used to count the days…' Nell shook her head at her own stupidity. 'It went on for six months and then he told me that he was married. He said it didn't matter, that he and his wife had some kind of understanding, but I broke it off immediately.'

Nell looked into Hugo's face, wondering if he could understand. 'I thought he loved me. And even though I loved him, I couldn't do it.'

'Sounds as if you were the one who was the adult in that relationship.'

He thought so? Nell had always considered herself as the silly little girl, blinded by love. Slowly Martin was developing feet of clay.

'I don't know about that. But I stuck to it, even though he contacted me a few times afterwards. Finally he left me alone, and I reckoned that it was just a life lesson and I should chalk it up to experience. I graduated, and got a job at the hospital and things were going well. Then the head of department retired, and…' Nell felt herself start to shake. That feeling, that she couldn't escape and that her mistakes would always come back to bite her, had turned out to be about the only true thing in this whole business.

'And when the new head of department showed up, it was him?' Hugo was filling in the gaps now. 'Any reasonable man would have spoken to you privately, admitted that he'd acted very badly and hoped that you might find the goodness of heart to draw a line under the whole business. I'm guessing he didn't do that.'

Nell shook her head, finding herself smiling grimly. 'No, he didn't. There were a couple of weeks of extreme awkwardness, and then I couldn't bear it any longer. I spoke to him and apologised…'

'*You* apologised?'

'It seemed reasonable. I had been one very willing half of the affair.'

Hugo let out a short, sharp breath. 'Are you saying it was all your fault?'

'No, I…' In truth, after the last six months, Nell had been reduced to not knowing what was and wasn't her fault.

'We talked a bit and I thought we'd come to an understanding, but the following day he said he wanted to talk a bit more and could he meet me for coffee that evening.'

Nell still didn't understand how she could have been so stupid. But when she looked at Hugo, there was no sign of reproach in his face. Perhaps he was just waiting to hear everything before he made a final decision on that.

'I went, and he started telling me about how his marriage had broken up because his wife had found out about our affair. I don't know if that was true, but I was horrified. Then he said that the least I could do was give things another try. I said I didn't think that was a good idea and he offered to take me home. He walked me to my door and then he told me he knew I wanted it really and pushed me inside. Somehow I fought him off…' The words had tumbled out, and Nell was suddenly breathless with shame.

'I hope you hurt him.'

'I… Actually, I had a copy of *Welman's Clinical Procedures* in my bag. I managed to get free of him and hit him with it.'

Hugo grinned suddenly. 'Good girl. The full edition, I hope.'

'Stop it, it was the abbreviated edition. It still hurt him, though. He made some comment about my obviously not being in the mood tonight and left.' She was shaking. Not so much as she had that night, but she still couldn't stop.

'Did you report him?'

'No, I…' Nell shrugged miserably. 'I was the one who asked him in. And it wasn't as if we'd just met, we had a history.'

'No means no. Nothing trumps that.'

It seemed so simple when he said it like that. Hugo's sense of honour made it simple. She wished that he'd reach out to her, but knew that he wouldn't. As far as Hugo was concerned, one touch now would make him as bad as Martin and she wished she could find a way to tell him that wasn't true.

She had to finish the story. Get this over with as quickly as possible. If she could do it without breaking down, that would be a bonus. Nell squeezed her hands together in her lap, feeling her nails dig deep.

'He…tried it on a few times after that. I rejected him and started to make sure we were never alone together. Then one day he called me into his office, and went through a very comprehensive list of all the things I was doing wrong. All from a clinical point of view, there was nothing personal.'

'Payback time?'

'Yes. That went on for a few months, and I started to wonder whether there really was something wrong with the way I did my job. Then he blocked my promotion.'

'On what grounds?'

'He said I was an excellent doctor but that realising my full potential meant staying in my current post a little while longer.' If Martin had criticised her performance, Nell could have fought it. But this had been impossible.

Hugo thought for a moment. 'He's done this before.'

'What? What makes you say that?'

'He always put you in a position where you felt you were in the wrong, he was married, then his divorce was because of his relationship with you. And he was always in a position of power, your teacher, and then your boss. I'm not saying he engineered all that, but he exploited it. He's an abuser, and he probably didn't just do it to you.'

'But…' Nell had thought she was alone. The idea that Martin might have done this to other women was horrific, but it did make her feel as if it wasn't so much her fault. 'Maybe you're right.'

Hugo got to his feet, starting to pace. 'We're going to stop him, Nell. My mother will refute the allegations and we'll release the details of my operation. That'll keep the papers busy for a while, and in the meantime we'll find a way to shut him up permanently.'

'No, Hugo. I know that's not what you want, and this is *my* battle. You shouldn't be dragged into it…' The heat in her heart, at the idea that Hugo was prepared to defend her, was burning too hot and threatened to consume her. He couldn't be allowed to do this.

'It's what works.' Hugo had obviously made his mind up about this.

'No, it won't work. Martin will just find another way to make these allegations…' If Hugo was so determined to make this sacrifice, Nell needed to find a different approach.

'If he does, then we're in a good place to refute them.' A grim smile quirked his lips. 'You underestimate the power of good contacts.'

'It's not about having power, Hugo, it's about what's right and wrong.'

He shook his head slowly. 'It's about picking a side, Nell. Allow me to pick mine.'

She stared at him. Hugo was on her side. The thought that he would protect her washed every objection she had to the idea away for a moment. He took full advantage of that moment, turning and walking out of the apartment.

It was done. Hugo had spent an hour with his mother and the palace press advisor, and a call had been made to the managing editor who had contacted them for comment. The promise of a press release within the next twenty-four hours had oiled the wheels, and Martin Jarman's story was suddenly dead in the water.

'I'm proud of you.' His mother had stopped him as he'd gone to leave, murmuring the words.

'It's a matter of principle.' Hugo had been telling himself that. He was doing this for everyone caught in this kind of situation, and not just for Nell. Not because he wanted to hold her close and keep her safe.

'Yes, it is. Anyone in your position has a duty to defend someone who...' His mother paused. 'You are quite sure that Nell is innocent of these allegations, aren't you?'

'Of course I am. I'm perfectly capable of noticing when a woman is trying to seduce me. Nell's a good doctor, and she acts appropriately.' His thoughts might touch on the delights of the inappropriate from time to time, but that was his business.

His mother nodded. 'Your judgement is always sound, Hugo. And whatever you say, I'm still proud of you.'

That was something. Hugo reflected that he wasn't all that proud of himself at the moment. The idea of having his most humiliating secret blazoned across the front pages of the papers was something he was trying not to think about. While he was still obviously recovering, people might look at him with sympathy. But sooner or later, they'd come around to seeing him as a hypocrite. How could he advocate for a heart clinic when he—a doctor no less—hadn't seen the signs of his own heart issues?

That was just something he'd have to put up with. Maybe Nell was right. Maybe an admission that he'd made the mistakes that he was urging others not to make would emphasise his human side. But right now Hugo's human side was cowering somewhere in a corner, and it felt far more comfortable to pretend that there was nothing wrong with him.

He walked back to his apartment, pondering the question. Things had to change—there would be no more battles of will with Nell, no more creative solutions. Even though the alternative sounded dull in the extreme, their relationship from now on would be entirely professional. If he were blameless, that would give Nell the opportunity to prove herself blameless, too.

Nell had waited for Hugo in his apartment. She'd made a cup of coffee, leaving it untouched while it had gone cold, and then emptied and washed the cup. Then she'd retreated to her own apartment, leaving the connecting door wide open, and switched the television on, hoping it might drown out the clamour of her own thoughts.

This was wrong. She'd been unable to say conclusively that she was entirely blameless in the business with Martin, but Hugo was different. No part of this was his fault, and yet in defending her he was the one who would feel humiliated.

Nell thought for a long time. When he came back, she'd put a stop to all this.

She heard the front door of his apartment close quietly, and hurried to the connecting door, stopping short at the threshold. When Hugo walked into the sitting room and saw her, he smiled.

Nell imagined that this was the smile he reserved for the most formal of occasions, devoid of any emotion other than the one he wanted to project. 'It's done, Nell. I'm going to...get some rest now.'

Normally she would have applauded the sentiment. Now, keeping Hugo awake until he'd told her exactly what had been done, and how it could be unravelled, seemed far more important.

'What's done?'

'Our press officer has stopped the story. We've promised a press release on another matter during the next twenty-four hours.'

Things had moved faster than Nell had thought they might. But it still wasn't irrevocable. 'We can undo it then. I can find another way.'

He paused for a moment, just long enough for Nell to wonder whether he was reconsidering. But he was just choosing his words. 'As I said, Nell, this is my battle too, and you don't have to find another way.'

This was too much. Standing, yards away from each other, trading appropriate conversation. They should be past this by now, but somehow Martin had inveigled his way in between them, and Hugo no longer felt comfortable with the relationship they'd started to build.

It was obvious that Hugo wasn't going to ask her into the apartment, but she couldn't say what she wanted to say from the doorway. Nell took the initiative, walking over to the sofa and sitting down.

'What did your mother mean by the Royal Agreement?' Hugo had dismissed the idea quickly, but maybe this was an alternative.

He shook his head. 'It doesn't apply here. When my parents were first married, they were keen to bring up their family without the constant press attention that my father had when he was young. They made an agreement

with the press, and until I was eighteen, the only news
stories published about me were official press releases
from the palace.'

Nell frowned. That didn't seem to apply, but Queen
Margaux had obviously thought it did. 'There's something
you're not telling me.'

'My mother showed a great deal of foresight in negotiating certain extensions to that protection. My grandmother
was allowed privacy during her final illness. And an engaged couple can expect the same privacy.'

An engaged couple?

What was the Queen thinking? Nell swallowed down
her own objections to the plan, because it was something,
anything, that would provide an alternative to what Hugo
was planning to do now.

'So your mother's suggesting that…if we got engaged
then there would be no difficulty in stopping this and other
stories about us.'

'Yes, that's exactly what she's suggesting. But I won't
put you through that…'

'You make it sound as if you're committing me to the
palace dungeons. It's not as bad as that, is it?'

The flicker of a smile crossed his face. 'No. Not quite.'

'Well, can't we consider it? I don't have to actually
marry you, do I?'

'No, you don't. We'd have to make a show of being together for a few months, but after that we'd break the engagement off quietly… But look, Nell, your career is at
stake here. There's no point in saving it, only to have it
ruined by being engaged to me.'

He had a point. Leaving her job and getting engaged to
a prince might not look great on her CV, but it wouldn't be
as disastrous as having Martin's story in the papers, and
it wouldn't hurt Hugo as much as his current plan would.

'I don't have to spend all my time just pretending to be

engaged, do I? I could do some work with your charity, if that's okay with you.' He shook his head and Nell puffed out a breath. 'This isn't doing my ego any good, Hugo. Is it that bad to have to pretend you're engaged to me?'

He laughed suddenly, all his reserve dissolving in his smile. 'I'd be very honoured to be engaged to you. Even if I was just pretending.'

'Then stop this nonsense about having to release the private details about your surgery. It's not necessary, we can find another way.'

Nell had started to boss him around again and his resolve to keep her at a distance had melted. But at least she didn't seem so beaten and dejected as she had when she'd recounted how she'd been treated by her last boss.

He'd begged her not to go through with this, and had told her that it was no sacrifice to allow his own medical details to be released to the papers instead, but she'd seen straight through him. So he'd called his mother, hoping that she might regret her mention of the Agreement, and talk some sense into Nell.

Fat chance. His mother had made a comment to the effect that she wished he'd make up his mind, and had gone on to embrace the idea. She appeared at the door of his apartment within minutes, and it seemed that she saw eye to eye with Nell over this compromise solution.

The details were worked out over a glass of wine. Nell insisted on giving up her employment, which seemed only sensible to Hugo. He insisted on her being involved with his work for the clinic as much as possible, so she'd at least have something to show on her CV later on. Even if that hadn't worked out so well with his real engagement to Anna, it seemed that it could at least be accomplished in the context of a fake engagement.

'This will work well, Hugo. You're obviously already

good friends.' His mother's habit of not leaving before she'd
made some private comment about the situation could be
trying, even if it did usually elicit her real thoughts.

'We're...' Hugo shrugged. '*Good friends* doesn't happen in the space of four days.' Even if it did feel as if he'd
known Nell for much, much longer than that.

'You want to protect her. She wants to protect you.' His
mother turned on her heel, leaving Hugo to think about
the implications of her statement.

He was too tired to think about anything very much.
Nell cleared away the glasses, and thankfully skipped any
examination of the healing incision on his chest. Perhaps
she knew that the intimacy would be too much for him to
bear tonight, when he was fighting to remain detached,
now that they were alone.

He slept deeply, not remembering his dreams. In the
morning, a package sent from his mother set the seal on
the agreement that had been made last night, which was
itself the stuff of crazy dreams.

He tore open the package and, looking inside, found a
short handwritten note from his mother.

Treat her with the greatest respect, Hugo.

Right. He didn't need to be told. He reached into the
envelope again, finding a bundle of tissue paper wrap-
pings and another note. He looked at both briefly, before
putting them in his pocket.

CHAPTER EIGHT

NELL HEARD THE knock on the connecting door between their apartments, just as she was putting the last of her clothes into her suitcase. When she answered it, Hugo was looking rested, which was a great deal more than she felt.

'You've had breakfast?' He grinned at her and she felt her stomach lurch. That would have been entirely appropriate if the engagement they were planning wasn't all a fabrication.

'No, I've been packing my bags. I was going to get that done first.' They'd agreed last night that it would be best for them both to leave the palace. Hugo's house in the country had no staff and was small enough that Ted and his team could maintain close security.

'Would you like to join me, then?'

She nodded. 'Yes. That would be nice, thank you. Just toast…'

An awkward silence accompanied the arrival of the tray from the kitchen, and Hugo motioned towards the balcony table, indicating that the tray should be set down there. Nell sat down, reaching for the coffee and pouring it.

'You still want to go through with it?' He didn't need to say what.

'Yes, I do. I'm even more sure this morning.'

He nodded, taking a tissue paper package from his pocket, undoing it and laying four rings in a line on the table. 'These are my mother's. She'd like you to have something nice to wear.'

In Nell's book, *something nice* didn't necessarily have to cost as much as the average house. 'They're real?'

'Yes, of course they are.'

'I can't wear any of these, Hugo, they must be worth… I can't even think how much they might be worth. Can't I wear a fake?'

He shook his head. 'No fakes, Nell, please. This engagement may not be real, but I want to say to you now that my promise to protect you is. I believe that you want to protect me, too.'

It wasn't the proposal that every girl dreamed of. But suddenly Nell felt that there was something real about this. Hugo was a better man than she'd thought he was, not just a spoiled prince who could destroy her if he wanted, the way that Martin had tried to.

'I will protect you, Hugo. I promise you that.'

He nodded. 'Then I'd like it if you would choose whichever ring you like the best.'

That sounded like something she could put her heart into. She looked at the rings, not daring to touch any of them. One had a massive ruby at the centre, and it looked far too opulent. The other three were all large diamonds.

'That one…' She pointed awkwardly to a diamond solitaire that flashed blue-white in the morning sunshine.

'That's a very good choice. It's the best stone.'

Nell went to protest that the only thing she'd seen was that it was the smallest stone, and he silenced her with a laugh. Picking up the ring, he held it out towards her. 'Will you wear it now?'

'The announcement hasn't gone out yet. I shouldn't wear it until tomorrow, should I?'

'We've made a promise. I'd like it if you would wear

the ring now, because that's what it is to us. You can wear it on your right hand until tomorrow.'

Still he wouldn't touch her. It was as if this new arrangement had blotted out any possibility of an innocent touch, and anything physical was now laden with some kind of meaning. Nell reached out, putting her hand in his.

'Then…would it be appropriate for you to put it on for me, please?'

'I think that would be entirely appropriate.' His voice sounded inappropriately husky, and Nell avoided his gaze. Looking into his eyes wasn't necessary.

She felt him slip the ring onto her finger, twisting it a quarter turn to get it past the knuckle. 'It looks nice.'

Nice was a bit of an understatement. It looked amazing, and far too good for Nell.

'It's beautiful. I'll take care of it and return it to your mother in good condition.'

He wrapped the remaining three rings in the crumpled tissue paper, and then put them back into his pocket, withdrawing a piece of folded notepaper. He handed it to Nell and got to his feet. 'I'll leave you to read that.'

Nell read the note. Queen Margaux would be most grateful if she could accept whichever ring she and Hugo chose, as a gift. It would be a symbol of gratitude and of enduring friendship between them.

Nell put the letter down on the table. It was too generous, and she'd have to ask Hugo if there was some way she could express her gratitude to his mother, whilst refusing the gift. She had the feeling that wearing it after the arrangement was over wasn't going to be a particularly comfortable option.

But while she had it on her finger, she'd do her best for Hugo. She'd take care of him, and help him raise the money he needed for the clinic. That was a promise.

* * *

Hugo was aware that this arrangement had to be treated with the utmost delicacy. He must show how much he valued Nell as a friend. Slipping into anything more would be horribly easy, and something that he had promised himself he wouldn't do.

All the same, their departure from the palace seemed like the start of something new and exciting. With the top of his convertible rolled back, and Nell at the wheel, it felt as if he was making an escape with a beautiful woman at his side. Who knew what might happen when they were finally alone, away from the bustle of the palace?

Ted's voice from the back seat jerked him back into reality. 'Left-hand side…'

Nell obligingly swerved to the left of the palace driveway, and came to a halt, waiting for the palace guard to open the gates.

'Thanks. I nearly forgot.'

She waved to the guard, the ring flashing bright on her finger. Then she turned out of the gates into the anonymity of the busy city on a warm summer's morning.

Their destination was only half an hour's drive away, which was about as far as anyone could go from the capital of Montarino and still remain within its borders. There was no suburban sprawl, just a sudden change from houses to open countryside. And the countryside in Montarino *was* beautiful.

Hugo directed Nell through rolling hills and around the edge of a wide, blue lake. Another mile and they reached a high wall, built of weathered bricks, driving the length of it until they reached an archway, protected by a heavy wooden gate.

The gate swung open and Ted got out of the car, speaking briefly to the man who had opened it. He waved the car through, and Nell drew up outside the house. It was small by the standards of the palace, built in stone and shaded by trees. A small garden at the side was overlooked by arches, the weathered stone now housing state-of-the-art single sheets of glass.

'It's lovely. This has been in your family for a long time?'

Hugo quirked his lips downwards, shaking his head. 'No. I bought this place with my doctor's salary. Since I have almost everything else provided for me, it seemed like a good idea to have my own bolthole.'

Nell wondered what it must be like to have to take your own independence that seriously. She took it for granted that everything she had was the product of her own work, but Hugo seemed to need to make a distinction between what he'd been given and what he'd earned.

Inside, the house was light, airy and simple. None of the folderols of the palace, just plain furniture in neutral colours, exposed wooden beams and a utilitarian kitchen. Upstairs, there were three bedrooms, one of which was clearly Hugo's. He directed her towards a second, which commanded stunning views of the hills stretching off into the distance.

'I suppose I'll have to keep away from the windows when the news breaks.' Nell wasn't exactly sure what to expect.

'Not really. Because of the Agreement, the paparazzi won't be able to sell any pictures they take, so it's not worth their time. And Ted's team will make sure that no one disturbs us here.'

'You usually have this much security?' Nell had counted four men outside.

'No, it's usually just Ted, and he generally doesn't have all that much to do. He stays in the guest house at the back.'

Nell walked over to the window, looking out. Beyond

the garden, and shielded by trees, was a small cottage, nestling against the perimeter wall.

'It all sounds reassuringly normal.'

'Not quite. But we try to make it so.' Hugo was watching her speculatively. 'There is one thing I want to ask you.'

'What's that?'

'Nadine, the little girl in the brochure, wearing a pink dress. I told you she'd had an operation recently...'

'Yes, I remember.'

'Dr Bertrand, the head of department, is the only one there who knows that I've been ill—everyone else thinks I'm taking a leave of absence for fundraising. He told me that he'd have me removed by security if I went in to see Nadine earlier than seven days after my own operation.'

Nell grinned. 'He sounds like a good man...'

'He's a very good man. You'd like him.'

'And since this is the seventh day, you'd like to go and see Nadine.'

'It would be best to go today. After the news of our engagement breaks, my turning up on the ward might cause a bit of a stir.'

'Where is the hospital?'

'On this side of the city, so it'll only take twenty minutes to get there. I'm feeling better every day, and I'd really like to see Nadine.'

If this was normal, then it was a new normal that Nell hadn't experienced before. Hugo asking her whether or not he could do something. 'It sounds like a lovely idea. May I come along? I'd like to see the hospital.'

Hugo smiled. As time went on that smile was surfacing more and more, and it convinced Nell that everything was going to be all right. 'I was hoping you might. You'll have to drive.'

CHAPTER NINE

NO ONE SEEMED to notice Hugo's presence as they walked through the reception area at the hospital. He exchanged smiles with the receptionist at the main desk, who waved him through in much the same way as she probably would have done with anyone else she knew. Here, Hugo appeared to shed the mantle of royalty.

He led her through a maze of corridors, mysterious box in hand, and a high-speed lift took them to the seventh floor. Hugo punched a code into a keypad at the entrance to one of the wards and the doors opened automatically, allowing them through.

This might just be Hugo's greatest test. Fooling a group of luncheon diners that there was nothing wrong with him was one thing. Fooling a senior nurse was quite another, and just such a person had looked up from her conversation at the nurses' station and was heading straight towards them.

'Hugo. This is unexpected.' The woman spoke in French.

'I've come to see Nadine. This is Dr Nell Maitland, she's a cardiac specialist from London. Nell, this is Senior Nurse Adele LeFevre.'

Adele smiled, holding out her hand to Nell and switching to English. 'I'm pleased to meet you. I hope you see much that you like here.'

'I have already. This is a beautiful hospital.'

'Thank you. We are proud of it. When the new cardiac unit is built, we will be even more proud.' Adele's English was almost perfect, like that of so many of the people of Montarino. And she was keeping hold of Nell's hand, staring at her.

'I called Dr Bertrand to let him know we were coming. Is he free?' Clearly Hugo didn't expect everyone here to drop what they were doing as soon as he arrived.

'He is finishing his rounds.' Adele barely seemed to glance at Hugo. 'Ten minutes.'

'Very well. May I show Nell around, and then go to see Nadine?' He had the grace to ask that as well.

'Of course.' Adele flashed Nell a smile and turned back towards the nurses' station.

They walked through the cardiac unit, and Hugo showed her the light-filled wards, exchanging greetings with some of the nurses as they went. There were treatment rooms and a small sitting room with a dining room to one side for ambulatory patients. Everything was gleaming and state of the art, but Nell could see that the unit was working at its full capacity, with no empty beds in any of the wards.

'Why is everyone staring at me?' Nell whispered to Hugo as he punched a number code into a keypad next to the door at the far end of the ward.

'This is the first time I've ever brought a friend here.' He turned to her, looking a little sheepish.

So this was a first taste of the interest that would be shown in her, then, after the press release went out. Nell had anticipated something of the kind, but she hadn't expected to feel so exposed, as if she wanted to cling to Hugo for shelter.

'I suppose…if they're staring at me, then at least they're not looking at you. A lot less chance of anyone noticing that you're still recovering from an operation.'

'There is that.' He leaned closer, his arm moving protectively around her but not touching her. 'There's still time to change your mind. The press release won't go out for another couple of hours.'

Maybe this was why he'd wanted her here with him. To give her one last chance to back out of the engagement.

'I'm not changing my mind, Hugo. I've got the ring now.' She'd be wearing it on her left hand and not her right tomorrow. But today it meant the same as it would tomorrow, a symbol of their agreement to protect each other.

'Thank you for wearing it…' He reached out, as if to take her hand, and Nell heard a stifled giggle coming from somewhere behind them. Two young nurses were at the other end of the corridor, staring at them. Adele bore down on them, shooing them back to work, and then shot a smile in Nell's direction.

Hugo ushered her through the door and one look told Nell that this was the children's ward. There was a riot of colour on the walls of the reception area and an open door revealed a play area, where young patients were being supervised by play leaders in bright tunics.

Hugo led Nell into a small ward, nodding a greeting to the nurse. Nell recognised the little girl who lay in one of the beds, as well as the teddy bear at her side.

'Hey, Nadine.' He dangled his fingers over the safety rail on the side of the bed, tapping the back of her hand, and she opened her eyes.

'Uncle Hugo.'

'I told you I'd come. I brought you something.' He opened the box he was carrying and drew out a beautiful silk flower, dangling it over the rail so that Nadine could see it.

'Thank you, Uncle Hugo.'

Nadine smiled, but didn't reach for the flower. Nell saw concern in Hugo's eyes and she knew what he was about to do next.

'Speak to Dr Bertrand,' she whispered in his ear and he ignored her.

'How do you feel, sweetie?' He reached forward to brush her forehead with his fingertips.

'I'm all right, Uncle Hugo.'

Hugo went to reach for the notes at the end of the bed, and Nell bowed to the inevitable and fetched them for him. 'I'm just reading about you.' He smiled at Nadine and she gave him a smile back.

He studied the notes carefully, and then checked the monitors by Nadine's bedside. From what Nell could see, everything was completely normal, and Nadine was just a little drowsy.

Hugo wasn't giving up, though. He reached for the sheet covering Nadine's body, pulling it back slightly to reveal her shoulders and a large plaster over the right side of her chest.

'No, Hugo. You are not to examine that child. You're on sick leave.' He'd probably survive, but goodness only knew what kind of medical liability issues it might raise.

'There's clearly something the matter with her.' He reached for a pair of surgical gloves from the dispenser on the wall, wincing slightly.

'Then we'll call for a doctor.' Nell beckoned to the nurse, asking her in French to fetch someone.

'I'm a doctor. Nadine is my patient.' She could hear the pain in Hugo's hushed voice, and Nell wondered what she'd do in his shoes.

'All right. Out of the way, I'll do it.' She grabbed the surgical gloves, pulling the heavy ring from her finger and putting it into his hand. Nell wasn't entirely sure what kind of liability issues that might also raise, but at least she was officially fit and well. And the thought that Hugo knew Nadine, and his instinct told him there was something wrong, was nagging at her.

'Thank you.' His green eyes flashed with warmth, and he turned to Nadine. 'Sweetie, this is Dr Nell. She's my friend.'

He stepped back but Nell could feel his eyes on her as she carefully moved the sheet that covered Nadine's chest further down. Everything seemed fine. The dressings were clean and there was no blockage that Nell could see in the surgical drain. When she gently touched Nadine's skin, it was cool.

All the same, she took the thermometer from the cabinet by the bed, inserting it carefully into Nadine's ear. The little girl was watching her solemnly. Nell looked at both her hands, and even her feet, for some sign that something might be wrong.

'I don't know, Hugo. I can't find anything.'

'Okay. We should try Claude.' He nodded towards a teddy bear propped up at the side of the bed.

Nell picked up the teddy bear. 'Hey, Nadine. Is Claude all right?' She spoke slowly, in French.

Nadine shook her head.

'No? Will you tell me what's wrong with him? I'd really like to make him better.'

'He has a pain.'

It was too much for Hugo. He moved in close and Nell shooed him back, out of the way. She leaned over the bed, holding Claude where Nadine could reach him. 'Where does Claude have a pain, Nadine?'

'There.' Nadine traced her finger over Claude's chest. Out of the corner of her eye, Nell could see Hugo flipping through Nadine's notes again.

'She's been having pain relief regularly. Not as much as she might, and my guess is that she's been telling everyone that it doesn't hurt. Nadine will do that.'

'Don't the nurses know?'

'They should. But the nurse who usually looks after her

is on holiday at the moment. I was supposed to be here.'
Nell heard Hugo's voice crack suddenly.

There was no answer to that, other than to remind Hugo
that he'd been under orders to stay away. Nell smiled at
Nadine. 'Uncle Hugo's going to find someone to make
Claude better.'

'Thank you, Dr Nell.' Nadine spoke slowly, her eyelids
drooping. Nell arranged the sheet carefully back over her
and stripped off her gloves. When she turned to follow
Hugo, she found that he was already gone.

She caught up with him, deep in conversation with another doctor, an older man. This must be Dr Bertrand. Nell
wondered whether Hugo was admitting that they'd carried
out a brief examination of Nadine, and guessed he probably wasn't. Dr Bertrand was nodding, and he turned to
walk quickly back to the ward with Hugo.

It was all worked out in the space of a couple of minutes. Dr Bertrand examined Nadine, listened to what she
had to say about how Claude was feeling and spoke to one
of the nurses, who hurried away.

Dr Bertrand gestured to Hugo, motioning him out of the
ward. He clearly had more to discuss, but Hugo seemed
reluctant to leave Nadine.

'I'll sit with her.' Nell plumped herself down on the
chair next to Nadine's bed, holding her hand over the guard
rail and feeling the little girl squeeze her fingers. Hugo
shot her a smile, and followed Dr Bertrand out of the ward.

By the time Dr Bertrand returned, a nurse had given
Nadine the extra medication, and she seemed a little happier, declaring that Claude felt better now. He spoke briefly
to Nadine and then pulled up a chair next to Nell.

'I gather that you too are a doctor.' Dr Bertrand spoke
in studied, careful English.

'Yes, that's right. I'm sorry, I know that this is highly
irregular...'

Dr Bertrand smiled. 'I have known Hugo for some years. His talent for being highly irregular, when circumstances require, is what helps make him one of my best doctors. This little one is feeling better now, and I have made sure that this will not happen again. Her nurse says that she was not in pain twenty minutes ago, on her last half-hourly check.'

'We just came at the wrong time, then.'

'No, it was quite the right time. If we can spare Nadine ten minutes of discomfort, then we are grateful. I have told Hugo that I cannot have him working while he is certified as sick.'

'How did he take that?'

'He has apologised and the matter is closed.' Dr Bertrand regarded Nell thoughtfully. 'He has many responsibilities, and is under a great deal of pressure. More than most men would be able to deal with.'

'Do you have any advice for me, Dr Bertrand?' Nell wanted to hear what this kindly, perceptive man had to say.

He leaned forward, as if he was about to impart some gem of wisdom. 'No. I do not.'

Nell had to think for a moment before she got the point. 'We all have to find our own way?'

'If anyone can, Hugo will.'

'Thank you.' Nell got to her feet, shaking his hand. 'May Hugo come to say goodbye to Nadine? He'll be no more than five minutes, I promise.'

'You will give him five, and he will take ten. And that is quite all right.' Dr Bertrand smiled at her.

One of the nurses directed Nell to Hugo's office and she found him sitting behind the desk, staring out of the window. She sat down and waited for him to say something.

'You don't need to tell me. I know I was wrong.' He didn't look at her.

'Yes, you were. For all the right reasons, though.'

'I know that Nadine's well cared for…' He swung his chair around to face her, and Nell saw that his face was full of anguish.

'But you can't help feeling that this is all your fault. For not being here.'

'I know it doesn't make much sense.'

'What happened, Hugo? When you were taken ill?'

'You know what happened. It's all in my notes.'

'I want to hear it from you.'

He frowned. 'You're psychoanalysing me?'

'No, I'm off duty, on account of an impending engagement.'

'Same as me, then. On account of not following my own advice.'

'So what happened?'

Hugo sighed. 'I knew my heart rate was lower than it should have been. And when I was in bed at night, I could…feel an irregular beat. I thought it might just be stress or overwork.'

'But it wasn't.'

'No. Surprisingly enough, despite being not only a doctor but also a prince, I couldn't just snap my fingers and tell myself to get better.' His voice was laden with heavy irony.

'And then you collapsed,' Nell prompted him for the next part of the story.

'Yes. Pretty much as detailed in my notes.' He shot her an exasperated look. 'Apparently my heart started beating again of its own accord, but when I was monitored overnight in the hospital, they found that it was beating too slowly and actually stopped every now and then.'

'How long for?'

'You know that, Nell. Up to three minutes. Which was almost enough to kill me if it wasn't corrected.'

'So they inserted a pacemaker. Which will help you live a completely normal life.'

'I don't *feel* normal, Nell.' He shook his head. 'It seems I'm not that good at coming to terms with my own flaws.'

'A pacemaker isn't a flaw, it's what makes you well.' So many pacemaker patients connected their device with the illness that had made it necessary. It was an obvious piece of logic, but it didn't help much when it came to accepting that their heart now needed a little help in order to function properly.

'I don't *feel* well. My shoulder aches still, I run into a brick wall whenever I try to do more than take life at a snail's pace... I can't even be at work, Nell. You see my desk? They've cleared it and given my cases to other doctors.'

'So you got sick. And you need a bit of time to get better. You're not superhuman and you're not perfect. Welcome to the world, Hugo. It's a place where pink marshmallow hospitals get built for little girls because only an imperfect world has the imagination to create that.'

Nell stopped, a little breathless. She wondered whether she might be accused of bullying a sick man, in a hospital of all places. You could probably get struck off for that kind of thing.

'You're sure about that?' He was looking at her solemnly.

'Yes, I'm sure. We're going to get the money you need.' Somehow, somewhere Nell had found a commitment to that.

He felt in his pocket, bringing out the ring. With everything else that had been going on, Nell had forgotten about it, and she was glad he hadn't lost it. She held her right hand out and he slipped it onto her finger.

'I feel... Sometimes I can't help listening to my heart, just to see if it's still beating. I'm not sure it's even possible, but I'd swear I feel the pacemaker kick in at times. It's as if my body isn't quite my own any more.'

He'd found a place where he could voice how he felt. There was still a journey ahead, but he'd found the starting point. 'That must be really hard for you. But in time, I promise you'll forget you even have it.'

Hugo nodded, slowly. 'I'm being an idiot, aren't I?'

'Yes, since you mention it.' Nell looked at her watch. 'You have five minutes to say goodbye to Nadine. Then you're coming with me.'

CHAPTER TEN

HUGO LAY ON his bed, staring at the ceiling. He had slept a little after their return from the hospital and then lain awake, thinking mostly about how Nell was both magnificent and unstoppable when she was angry.

He could hear her clattering around in the kitchen downstairs. Hugo got up, walking slowly into the en suite bathroom to splash his face with water. The scar on his chest was still there, but the stitches would be out soon. It seemed somehow to be fading already.

'I think I might cook this evening.' He made sure that he spoke while he was still a good twenty feet away from her so as not to make her jump. All the same, she did jump, turning around and flushing a little when she saw him.

'You can cook?' She smiled suddenly.

'Of course I can cook. I know how to deal with all the appliances in this house. Even the vacuum cleaner.'

'Well you're not dealing with that for a while, vacuuming requires too much reaching. Although it's something I'd really like to see as soon as you're well enough.'

Hugo chuckled. Everything was going to be just fine. 'I *can* cook, though. You can help if you like, and get things out of the cupboards.'

'What were you thinking of cooking?'

'I do a mean lasagne. I asked Ted to get the ingredients when he went shopping this morning.'

'Okay. I do a pretty mean lasagne myself, so let's see what yours is like.' She grinned as she threw down the challenge. 'Perhaps Ted can give us his opinion.'

'I'll give him a call when dinner's ready.' Hugo opened a drawer and took out an apron. A number of people had said he was a good cook, but no one had ever accused him of being a tidy one.

Nell walked across the kitchen, taking the apron from his hand and unfolding it. Then she reached up, putting it over his head.

'Thanks.' Hugo wasn't sure he could reach behind him to tie the apron, and he wondered whether Nell would do that for him as well. And whether she'd do it the way a fi-ancée would, reaching around from the front, or whether she'd prefer to do it from the back, the way a doctor might.

She reached around from the front. Somehow she managed to do it while hardly touching him, but she was so close that Hugo caught his breath.

'I was thinking…' She'd tied the bow in the apron strings but she didn't step back.

'What were you thinking?' he encouraged as she tailed off.

'That… Well, if I were called upon to kiss you, in light of our announcement…'

If she felt able to do that Hugo wouldn't object in the slightest. 'You're not going to be called upon to do any-thing you don't want to, just for the sake of appearances. We'll just do the same as we've been doing up till now.' He wasn't in the habit of pawing women in public any-way, and the thought that Nell might not welcome it made it a complete no-no.

'So no kissing?' It was extremely gratifying that Nell looked almost disappointed. Hugo supposed that a woman might close her eyes and kiss someone while overlooking their other physical flaws.

'I'd be extremely happy if you kissed me. And extremely unhappy if you felt in any way pressured to do so.'

'I don't.' There was a mischievous glint in her eyes, which made Hugo's heart beat faster. 'I just wouldn't like to do it for the first time in front of a crowd of people.'

Before Hugo could think of a suitable reply, she'd raised herself up on her toes, planting a soft kiss on the corner of his mouth. For a moment, she stared up at him and then lowered her gaze shyly.

He wanted so badly for her to do that again. It had been just a moment and it hadn't felt real, but it still felt special. 'May I...put my arm around you?' Hugo decided that asking first would be the best course of action.

'Yes. I'd like that.'

He put his right arm gently around her waist, resisting the temptation to pull her hard against his aching body. Then Nell reached up suddenly, putting her left arm around his right shoulder, her fingertips touching the back of his neck.

It was delicious. If she'd thrown all her clothes off it could hardly be any more arousing than this. He felt himself trembling at her touch, all the more powerful because she was touching so little of him.

He saw her pupils dilate suddenly, and that small reaction almost made him choke with desire. Nell kissed him again, this time on the centre of his mouth, lingering just long enough for him to return the kiss.

Neither of them needed to say anything. Nell had to know how much he liked this. And it was very clear that she was enjoying it, too. Too far gone to even worry about whether she might feel his arousal if she got any closer, he tightened his arm around her waist.

She melted against him, as if it were the most natural thing in the world. Chemistry wasn't going to be a problem. Not kissing her again was...

It happened again, almost of its own accord. One moment their lips were tantalisingly close and the next Hugo was kissing her, and Nell was kissing him back. Soft and slow, as if to imply that perhaps there was control over it.

He thought he felt her lose control, her fingers tightening suddenly into a fist against his chest. Her heart beat against his and… That sudden feeling, as if the pacemaker had just kicked in to accommodate the screaming urge to take this as far as it would go, and then further. It reminded him that he couldn't. Not yet, and very probably not ever.

Hugo drew back slowly, planting a last kiss on her waiting lips. 'This is a role I'm not going to have any trouble with at all.' This was special, even if it did promise nothing.

'Me neither. I think we're good with that part of it.' She gave him a luminous smile as Hugo released her from their embrace, and turned back to the kitchen counter. 'Now. How about something a little more practical? Let's see if you really *can* cook.'

It was as if Hugo had swept her up and they'd danced together through the last ten days. Nell had reorganised his diary, and although Hugo had put up a few token objections, they'd always come to an agreement. Even the round of golf was made easier for him by giving up his own opportunity to play in favour of teaching his new fiancée.

She'd stayed close to him in public, the obvious implication that they were in love disguising the fact that she kept to his left, always protecting his arm and shoulder. When she leaned across to whisper in his ear, the words she breathed were questions about how he felt, and his smiling answer was often accompanied by the brush of a kiss.

Hugo's manners were impeccable, always making sure she was seated before he was, his hand guiding her when she was faced with a crush of people and didn't quite know which way to turn. And they managed to waltz through seemingly difficult obstacles. When a particularly heavy door blocked their path, and Nell stepped forward to heave it open, a smile flickered on Hugo's face. He bowed to her, catching her hand up to kiss it, and Nell made a mock curtsey. It seemed like the relaxed playfulness of new lovers, and not a concerned doctor making sure that Hugo came to no harm.

The ring on her finger still felt odd, but Nell was getting used to it. She was getting used to always being watched. And she was beginning to understand how Hugo felt. Living his life, all the highs and lows of it, at the centre of everyone's attention must be hard.

And now there would be another test. A private dinner at the palace, attended by the royal family of Montarino and visiting French and German ambassadors. It was an important occasion, and Hugo was expected to be there, which meant that Nell was expected to be with him.

The morning dawned fresh and clear, and they were on the road as soon as Nell had gulped down a cup of coffee.

'I'm a bit worried about this dress...' Nell frowned as she drove out of the gates of the house.

'It's no big deal. My mother's got it in hand.'

'That's what I'm worried about.' The thought of being closeted with the Queen and a personal stylist from the largest store in Montarino, who would be bringing a selection of suitable gowns for the evening, was frankly terrifying.

'They'll help you pick something nice. And my mother will have the jewellery to go with it, she's got something to go with everything.'

'I'm going to feel foolish, Hugo. I'm not used to wearing a lot of jewellery.'

'Fine. No big jewellery. Just tell them.' He grinned. 'Anything else you don't want?'

'No sequins. And no frills. Definitely no bows.'

'Sounds good to me. I doubt my mother will have frills or bows in mind either, she generally goes for a more classic look. You might have to mention your aversion to sequins, though. What about colour?'

Nell sighed. Hugo didn't sound as if he was taking this as seriously as she was. 'No pink. And definitely no yellow.'

'Right, then. You've practically picked your dress already.' He stretched his long legs into the footwell, obviously ready to move on and enjoy the drive.

Driving *did* calm Nell a little, but as soon as she reached the palace car park, her fears returned. Hugo seemed intent on hustling her through the corridors to his parents' apartment as quickly as possible.

The apartment was larger than his, and more lavish. His mother greeted them both with a kiss, and Hugo followed them through to her dressing room, sprawling onto one of the cream silk upholstered chairs.

'Hugo, darling. You have something to do…' Queen Margaux fixed him with a determined glare.

'Nothing that I can think of.'

'I'm sure you might think a little harder, then.' The Queen took the words out of Nell's mouth, and Hugo ignored her.

A rail-thin, elegant woman appeared, a couple of assistants behind her wheeling a rack full of dresses. In any normal circumstances, she looked as if she might have chased Nell away from the confection of silks and satins that were far beyond her purse, but she greeted Nell obsequiously.

An analysis followed of Nell's colouring and figure, both of which were apparently perfect. Nell shifted awkwardly from one foot to the other, and out of the corner of her eye she caught Hugo's grin.

'I think it all goes without saying, *Madame*, that my fiancée is perfect in every way.' He got to his feet, advancing towards the rail, and Queen Margaux shrugged, dropping into a seat to watch. Clearly the preferred course of action when Hugo was in one of these moods was to wait a while, to let it all blow over.

'Of course, Your Highness.' *Madame* smiled beatifically at Nell.

'Let's have a look at these…' He was shuffling through the dresses. 'No…no…no… What about this one, Nell?' He held up a dark blue dress and then shook his head. 'No, it's got a bow at the back.'

'Detachable, of course, Prince Hugo.'

'Oh. What do you think, Nell?' He turned to Nell, suddenly still. Somewhere, deep in his eyes, she saw that maybe this wasn't going to be as excruciating as she'd thought.

'It's…very nice.'

'Watered silk, Miss Maitland.' *Madame*'s voice held a tang of disapproval. Clearly *very nice* wasn't the right reaction.

'Hmm.' Hugo peered at the bow at the back of the dress and shrugged. 'Well, perhaps that can go on the "possible" pile.'

He looked around, obviously trying to decide where to put the dress, and *Madame* clicked her fingers. One of her assistants sprang to attention, wheeling an empty rail forward and taking the dress from Hugo.

'This one, Prince Hugo?' *Madame* tried to reassert herself, grabbing a fuchsia-pink sequined gown.

'My fiancée is a doctor, *Madame*, not the Christmas Fairy.'

'Hugo!' Queen Margaux had been watching quietly, but now murmured a reproach.

'Apologies, *Madame*. What do you think, Nell?'

'It's…not really my style.' Nell smiled apologetically at *Madame*, who pursed her lips. 'What about this one?'

'Very plain.' *Madame* took the dark green velvet dress from the rail. 'Of course, with Queen Margaux's emeralds, it would be most striking.' Nell's heart sank as *Madame* held the dress up against her.

Hugo shook his head. 'Better without. What is it you say, Mother, wear the dress and don't let the dress wear you?'

Queen Margaux stifled a laugh. 'Yes, exactly. When did you become so interested in women's couture, Hugo?'

'Nell's been teaching me all kinds of things,' he responded dryly, and his mother smiled. 'Let's put that with the "possibles" and leave the emeralds for later.'

They'd whittled the dresses down to four. Three blue and the green one, which *Madame* was obviously regretting putting on the rail to bring to the palace. Hugo was questioning *Madame* closely on the latest trends in menswear, which gave Nell a chance to slip away alone to put the first dress on. When she returned, *Madame* practically ran over to her, tugging unnecessarily at the bodice.

'Perfect…perfect.' She turned to Hugo as if Nell didn't exist, looking for his reaction.

'You like it, Nell?' Hugo's gaze found hers.

'It's…it looks beautiful.' Nell looked at her own reflection in the mirror. Was that really her? 'It's a little tight.'

'Form-fitting…' *Madame* murmured the words.

'I'd recommend breathing over form-fitting. Can you breathe, Nell? On a scale of one to ten.'

Nell grinned at him. 'About three and a half. Maybe only three if I'm sitting down.'

'Well, go and take it off quickly. Before I have to resuscitate you…'

* * *

The dress was chosen. Hugo had somehow managed to infer that the diamond earrings and bracelet that his mother was lending to go with it were all *Madame*'s idea, and she'd left, trailing the scent of slightly mollified disapproval in her wake. Queen Margaux had asked Hugo whether he was going to interfere when the hairdresser arrived, and he'd shrugged. Nell had laughingly told him that she thought she could manage alone.

'It's a matter of knowing your power.' Since the choosing of the dress had been accomplished in record time, they were now free until three o'clock, and Hugo had taken Nell for a stroll in the palace gardens.

'I'm not sure I have any power, do I?' Nell looked up at Hugo. Caressed by the sun and relaxed in the warm breeze, he seemed the epitome of a handsome prince.

'Of course you do. You know, when you're a prince, people will tell you that you're the one in charge. And then they tie you up in knots over all of the things you can and can't do.'

'Like having to accept your own private doctor?' Nell knew now that Hugo's studied avoidance of her advice hadn't been just a game. He'd been fighting to express his own feelings over his surgery.

'Well…that worked out. And you were right, I did need to rest a little more. And I needed to be told that I'm not indestructible.'

'You needed to accept that for yourself. Not to be told.'

He chuckled. 'Yes. Big difference. And you don't need to be told which dress you like, so remember that next time.'

'There probably isn't going to be a next time.' Nell had to remind herself every day that this wasn't permanent. That she wasn't really Hugo's fiancée and that in a few months' time she'd be leaving.

'No. I suppose not.' Suddenly the space between them seemed to grow. Their leisurely pace was the same, but they were just taking the same path through the gardens, not walking together.

'Thank you for stepping in, though. I'm not sure what I would have ended up with if you hadn't been there.'

'My mother knows how to handle *Madame* and her entourage. It might have deteriorated into a squabble, though.'

'A squabble? Surely not!'

Hugo chuckled. 'They've known each other for years. *Madame* has access to all the best dresses, but she's not that flexible in her approach. There have been a few full and frank discussions.'

'I didn't realise…'

'That's what I mean about taking your own power. People like *Madame* love to tell you what to do, but if you stand up to them, they've got nothing.'

'And you take a lot of pleasure in standing up to them, don't you?'

He didn't answer. The complex politics, the unspoken expectations of the palace must be hard to live with. Being a doctor seemed suddenly a lot simpler.

'I've been thinking. About Martin…'

He raised an eyebrow. 'Yes? You do that a lot?'

'Not all that much.' The last ten days had been busy. And full of the kind of achievement and joy that didn't naturally bring Martin to mind. But that respite had served to consolidate Nell's thoughts.

'I'm glad to hear that.' There was a note of possessiveness in Hugo's tone.

'I checked his social media accounts. He's been very quiet recently.' Nell had wondered whether Hugo had had anything to do with that.

'The email that our legal team sent him might have had something to do with that.'

'So you *did* do something.'

'Nothing very much. They simply made contact and made a polite request that any future public statements be copied to them, as a courtesy.'

'But coming from an eminent law firm, with the backing of the palace… That sounds like a threat to me.'

'There were no threats. All bullies are cowards, don't you know that? If Jarman backs off because you have powerful friends, that's his business.'

'I was thinking maybe…that I might make him back off by myself. I'm considering lodging an official complaint with the hospital.'

Hugo nodded. 'If that's what you want. It won't be easy, though. Our lawyers can support you through the process.'

'I know, but I don't want that. I thought about what you said, about him probably acting that way towards other people. I'd been so bound up in my own problems that I thought I was alone, but if there *is* anyone else…'

'You want to support them.' He clearly approved of that wholeheartedly.

'Yes, I do. And I want him to know that I did it alone. That I have the power to fight back by myself.'

'Okay. Does that mean I'm not allowed to help?'

'As a friend?' That was a far more demanding proposition. One word and he could have the weight of highly placed contacts and a hotshot legal team crashing down on Martin's head. It would take a lot more input from him to support her through the process as her friend.

'Yes. Always.'

'If I wrote everything down, would you be able to look through it? Give me your opinion?'

His hand drifted to hers, and he tucked it into the crook

of his elbow, his thumb brushing against the ring on her finger.

'Yes, of course. Partners.'

'Thank you. I'd like that.' The ring meant one thing to everyone else who saw it and quite another to her and Hugo. That they couldn't love each other but they could be friends, who protected each other.

CHAPTER ELEVEN

HUGO HAD LET her go, and Nell had set off for his parents' apartment with a hint of determination in her step. Whatever happened with her hair and make-up, he was pretty sure that Nell would have a say in it.

He took more time than usual dressing, his left arm still hampering him as he sorted through his wardrobe to find a waistcoat that was exactly the shade of the dress she'd chosen. He'd never done that before, not for any woman, but Nell… They were of the same mind. Beneath all their differences they were cut from the same cloth.

He heard her let herself back into his apartment and rose from his chair to meet her. A little thrill ran up his spine, tempered by a reminder to himself that he shouldn't expect too much.

And then, not expecting too much became irrelevant. He couldn't possibly have expected her to look this stunning. The slim-line green dress traced her curves, the hem high on her ankle. A slender row of diamonds at her wrist and neck and a pair of high-heeled, strappy shoes balanced the look perfectly.

'What do you think?' She was pressing her lips together, and Hugo realised that his over-awed silence had left Nell waiting a little too long.

'I think the dress is very nice.' He wanted to touch the soft folds of material, but instead he allowed his hand to trace the shape of her waist, just millimetres away from it. 'The diamonds are just right for it.'

She gave him a nervous smile and he permitted his fingers to follow the curve of her chin. Still not touching her. Somehow not touching was almost as sensual as feeling the softness of her skin. 'They'd be nothing without you, though. *You* are exquisite.'

'You think…it's all right?' She was smiling now.

'It's so much better than all right that…no, it's not just all right.'

Nell nodded, obviously pleased, walking over to where his jacket hung across the back of the chair. Picking it up, she helped him on with it, smoothing her hands across his shoulders.

'Will I do?' He smiled down at her.

'For an everyday, handsome prince? You'll definitely do.'

He made her feel good. Clinging to his arm had become a matter of each supporting the other now. Nell protected him from being bumped and jostled, and he protected her from the enquiring heads that turned to look her way.

Everything glittered, from the magnificent chandeliers high above their heads down to the jewels of the assembled company. The great and the good of Montarino, along with delegations from their neighbouring countries. Hugo passed effortlessly between them all, his arm always there for her, the place by his side always reserved for Nell.

The King and Queen led the way into the grand dining hall. Queen Margaux shone in a canary-yellow dress, which complemented her blonde hair, and King Ferdinand was upright and gracious beside her. Everyone was seated, and Nell looked around nervously, feeling Hugo's fingers brush hers under the snowy tablecloth. She looked into his smile and nodded an answer to his unspoken question. As long as she waited and followed his lead in picking the right one from the array of silver knives and forks in front of her, she'd be fine.

Hugo had taken charge of the conversation at their part of the table, asking questions and including everyone. Soon their group was animated and laughing and even Nell began to relax. Underneath the fine clothes and the magnificent surroundings, they were just people getting to know each other.

'Would you like a break?' As they rose from the table, Hugo bent towards her, murmuring in her ear.

'Can we…? Don't you have to stay with your guests?'

'My parents have it covered. Just for ten minutes, so that you can stop having to keep smiling.'

That would actually be nice. Nell's jaw was beginning to ache a little. She followed Hugo as he slipped through the open French doors and out onto the stone-flagged terrace. A number of people seemed to have had the same idea, and Hugo led her out of the circle of light cast by lanterns that were positioned around the terrace, down the steps and into the garden.

'You're *sure* we won't be missed?'

He chuckled. 'This is Montarino, not England. Protocol practically demands that a newly engaged couple disappear for at least ten minutes during the course of the evening.' Hugo walked slowly along the paved path, which was flanked by a sculpted hedge.

'Ten minutes. Not much time, then?' She grinned up at him.

'Something else you need to learn about Montarino. We know how to make very good use of just ten minutes.'

Suddenly ten minutes seemed like ten hours. Out here in the warm evening breeze, the lights and noise of the house were beginning to recede behind them. Nell shivered at the thought.

'Cold?'

'No, it's nice to be out here. It was beginning to get very hot inside.'

Their leisurely pace grew more leisurely, until they were standing together. She had to touch him. Nell ran her fingers down the lapel of his jacket and felt Hugo's hand resting lightly on her waist.

'So…while everyone thinks we've escaped to do what every engaged couple does…' Hugo chuckled.

'We could read the paper?'

'We could. Or play a game of cards.'

'Not enough time.' Nell reached up to touch his face. There was only one thing she really wanted to do right now. And since tonight was all about their public personas, an engaged couple who were naturally very much in love, maybe that one thing was permissible.

'No. You're right.' His gaze never left her face as he raised her hand to his mouth, kissing her fingers.

They could have stopped there. But Nell didn't want to, and she knew that Hugo didn't either. Ten minutes.

His lips were almost touching hers. This wouldn't be the formal kiss, planted on her cheek or hand, to delight the people around them. This was just for her.

Hugo's arm tightened suddenly around her waist and she felt his body tighten against hers. 'Who's there?'

There was a rustle in the bushes behind her. Hugo pulled her away, facing the hurried whispers coming from the darkness. And then a shape detached itself from the deepest of the shadows, followed by another.

'Who's there?' Hugo asked again, his tone demanding an answer.

'The necklace…' A low voice, full of menace, spoke in French and Hugo pushed Nell behind him. Not a good idea, even if he had been in full health. Nell kicked off her shoes, ready to run, clinging to Hugo's arm.

'All right.' He held one hand out in a gesture that was clearly intended to calm the situation.

'Quickly!' The man spoke again, taking another step forward. He was holding something in his hand, and Nell wondered whether he was armed.

This must have been so easy. Any one of the women here was wearing jewellery that would fetch a high price. The men had only to get through high railings at the perimeter of the palace, conceal themselves in the garden and then wait.

'Nell. Give me the necklace.'

'What?' Queen Margaux's diamond necklace. She'd promised herself to take good care of it. But if giving it up was unthinkable, the alternative was even worse.

She fumbled with the catch at the back of her neck, but it was too firmly secured for her trembling fingers. And she'd hesitated for a moment too long. The man lunged towards her as if to tear the necklace from her throat, and she felt Hugo's body pushing her back and taking the brunt of the impact.

'No…Hugo!' He was stumbling to one side and Nell cried out in terror. 'I'll give it to you.' She pulled frantically at the necklace, trying to get it off.

But it was too late for that. She felt a gloved hand close around her wrist, trying to get at her bracelet, and then she was free again as Hugo let out a great roar, tackling her assailant. The man lashed out at Hugo, and she saw a spark. In the silence, broken only by the sound of the wind in the trees, the clicking sound seemed to last for a very long time, even if it was just a few seconds. Then Hugo screamed in pain, dropping to the ground like a stone.

'Hugo!' There was no possibility of just giving the men what they wanted and letting them go now. Nell yelled for help at the top of her voice, hoping that if the assembled company in the palace didn't hear her, there would be a security patrol in the grounds that did.

The men were running now, and Nell dropped to her knees beside Hugo. He was still groaning and gasping for air, and she grabbed his arm, feeling for his pulse.

'Uh…' He tried to speak, but couldn't. All Nell could do was to hold him, as if that might absorb some of his pain into her own body and spare him.

'I know. He had a stun gun. They're gone now.' Nell knew that a jolt from a stun gun could disable the strongest man. It dealt excruciating pain, rather than injury, but a recent operation and a pacemaker complicated things.

Hugo knew that as well as she did. 'You're okay, Hugo. I can feel your pulse.'

His body relaxed a little, but there was still fear in his eyes. 'You're…sure?' His voice sounded thick and strange, and his free hand drifted to his chest.

'I'm sure. I feel it beating, Hugo. Strong and steady.' Fast. But who could blame it for that?

A noise behind her made her jump and Nell looked round to see three men from the palace security team. People were running down the steps of the terrace and Nell could see the King at their head, no longer the stiff monarch but a man of action like his son.

'I'm a doctor. Stand back, he's all right.' She waved the security men back, and they formed a triangle around them, keeping watch. Nell clung to Hugo, trying to comfort him, as he rolled painfully onto his back, his head in her lap.

'Hugo!' The King practically skidded to a halt, bending down, his questioning gaze meeting Nell's.

'He's been hit by a stun gun. It's very painful but it'll pass. The jolt from a stun gun shouldn't affect a pacemaker.' Her words were for Hugo, as much as they were for the King. It must have been terrifying, feeling only pain, his body out of control. Knowing that the pacemaker was there in his chest and wondering whether his heart had already stopped beating.

The King knelt down, suddenly just another father. 'You hear that, son?'

Somehow Hugo managed a smile. 'Never contradict a lady…'

'No. That's right.' King Ferdinand flashed a tight smile at Nell and reached for his son. Hugo took his hand, gripping it tight.

The King had asked one of the men who came running towards them to tell the Queen that Hugo was all right and then his attention was for Hugo alone. He hardly seemed to notice the security guard who had approached and was standing at a respectful distance, waiting to be acknowledged.

Nell caught the guard's attention, keeping her fingers on Hugo's pulse. Now wasn't the time to interrupt the King. 'You have something to report?'

'We've apprehended the two men, and called the police.'

'Thank you for acting so quickly. I'll tell the King. Do you have the stun gun?'

'Yes, ma'am.'

'Would you find out the make and model for me, please?' Obtaining the information would stop the guard from hovering here, and finding out exactly what Hugo had been hit with couldn't do any harm.

'Yes, ma'am.' The guard turned and hurried away.

Maybe she'd overstepped her authority, but there was no trace of reproof in the King's face when he looked up at her.

'Thank you, Nell. Should we move him, now?'

'I'd like to take Hugo to hospital. It's just a precaution, but I want a pacing check done, and he should be monitored for a little while. Just to be on the safe side.' Scar

tissue hadn't had a chance to form around the newly implanted leads yet, and they might have been dislodged
by the scuffle or the sudden convulsions of Hugo's body.

'I think that's wise.' The King nodded, looking down at
Hugo. 'What do you say, Hugo? Still in no mood to contradict the lady...?'

'No mood at all.' Nell had been sure that Hugo would
protest, but he just nodded. This had frightened him even
more than she'd thought. 'You should go back to our
guests, Father.'

For a moment the King seemed torn. Then he shook
his head.

'He'll be all right. And I'll keep you and the Queen in-
formed.' It seemed wrong to break the new bond that had
surfaced between father and son in the heat of this emer-
gency, but Nell was beginning to understand that duty was
a hard taskmaster.

'Every step of the way?' The King's voice was cracked
with emotion.

'Yes, I promise.'

The King bent over his son. 'You know we'll be there,
Hugo. Your mother and I...'

'Yes. Just give me a bit of space.' Hugo's words were
clearly a fond joke, and his father laughed quietly.

'Perhaps you'll help me get him up on his feet and we
can walk him over to the car.' Before now, Nell would
never have asked the King to do such a thing. But he
seemed to need this, and Hugo clearly did, too. It had taken
a stun gun and a lot of pain before the two men had been
able to bury their differences, but maybe it was worth it.

CHAPTER TWELVE

ALTHOUGH THE JOURNEY to the hospital was a short one, the car was starting and stopping in the evening traffic. Ted had been fetched from the palace kitchen and arrived stony-faced, clearly annoyed with himself that he'd done what had been expected of him and relied on the security measures at the palace to keep Hugo safe for the evening. He sat in the front seat of the car, next to the chauffeur.

'I feel fine now. There's no need for the hospital. Ted...?' Hugo appealed to the back of Ted's head from the back seat of the car, where he sat with Nell.

'You know what I think.' Ted didn't turn around, and Hugo looked across at Nell in a silent appeal.

'We're going to the hospital.' Nell glared at him. If he thought that she was an easier touch than Ted, he had another think coming.

'Yes, ma'am.' Hugo settled back into his seat. 'Only I'll prove you wrong when I get there.'

'That's exactly what I expect you to do. And it's never wrong to be on the safe side.'

She heard Ted chuckle from the front of the car, and Hugo rolled his eyes.

By the time they arrived at the hospital, the cardiac surgeon who had implanted Hugo's pacemaker had been roused from his bed. Nell quickly told him what had happened and he nodded in agreement with her assessment.

She left him alone with Hugo for a moment, and found Ted brooding outside the door.

'He's okay, Ted.'

'I know. But *I* should have been there. A stun gun hurts like the blazes.'

If Ted had been on duty, she and Hugo would have found a way to evade him. The sweet promise of those moments with Hugo, alone in the darkness, made Nell shiver. 'You can't be with him all the time. You were off duty.'

Ted knew that she was trying to make him feel better, and flashed her a wry smile. 'He knows what to do if there's an incident. He should stay back and shout for help.'

'He was protecting me.' Nell had been feeling just as guilty as Ted obviously was.

'Understandable.' The creases in Ted's forehead relaxed slightly. 'Maybe I'm getting a bit too old for this.'

Nell laid her hand on his arm. 'He trusts you, Ted. And Hugo needs people he can trust right now. I don't think age has anything to do with the fact that you can't be in two places at once.'

'Maybe…' Ted didn't look convinced, but at least he was thinking about it.

'Why don't you go and get a cup of tea? I'm sure there'll be somewhere…'

Ted nodded. 'The café on the ground floor is open all night. Would you like me to get you something?'

'No, I'll stay here and talk to his doctor. I'll call you when we've finished and you can see him.'

'All right.' Ted went to turn, and then stopped. 'Thanks.'

Hugo was lying in bed, a heart monitor by his side. His smile was back in full force, as his coping mechanisms kicked in.

'Don't you think this is a bit over the top? People get hit with stun guns all the time, and they get up and walk away.' He'd waited to come up with his objections until the door had closed quietly behind the cardiac surgeon.

'Yes, they do. But they're generally people in good health who haven't just had surgery. Give it a rest, Hugo.'

'I *am* in good health. Reasonable health, anyway. I'll feel better when I can get back into the gym.'

Nell rolled her eyes. 'Don't give me that, Hugo. This might be just a precaution but it's one that I believe is warranted, and your cardiac surgeon agrees with me.'

'I know what the risks are as well as you do…'

He broke off suddenly, seeing the tears that were filling Nell's eyes. This time she'd made no effort to hide them from him. Why should she? Nothing else seemed to get through to him.

'I'm sorry, Nell. I know you must have been really frightened tonight.'

'Yes, I was. And the bit that frightened me the most was hearing you scream and seeing you hit the ground.' She grabbed his hand, holding on to it tight.

He twisted his mouth down in a show of embarrassment. 'I heard that everyone cries like a baby when they're hit with a stun gun. I know why now…'

'Stop it, Hugo! Stop trying to make out that you weren't afraid. And don't pretend that your first thought wasn't that your heart had stopped, or that you needed your father and he was there for you.'

'Please… Don't cry.' His voice was suddenly husky.

'Well, someone's got to. Ted's maintaining a stiff upper lip, while wrestling with the idea that he should have been there. Your father was really cut up about letting you leave without him, but he had to put on a brave face for his guests. He really cares…'

'Yes, I know. I do too, we just… Sometimes we lose sight of that.' Suddenly he reached for her, shifting a little in the bed.

'Come here. Please… I need you, Nell.'

There wasn't a great deal of room on the bed but there was enough. Nell slipped off her shoes, lowering the bed a little and then climbing carefully up beside him. What the hell, if anyone found them like this, they were supposed to be engaged, weren't they?

He put his arm around her shoulders, holding her close. 'I couldn't protect you, Nell. I'm sorry.'

'I couldn't protect you either. And I'm sorry about that.' She nestled against him. Suddenly everything seemed all right.

They lay together for long minutes. No more words needed, just the silence and the feel of her heart beating. His, too. Finally Nell felt Hugo move, and when she looked up at him he brushed a kiss against her forehead.

'Much as I love having you here, you should go.'

'You're sending me away?' Perhaps Hugo felt he'd admitted a bit too much, and he wanted some time on his own to reconstruct his armoured exoskeleton.

'I can't sleep with you next to me. And you're going to need some sleep, too…'

'Me? I'm all right.'

Hugo chuckled. 'Don't you start. I'm all right enough for both of us. But I need you to do something for me.'

'What?' Right now, she just wanted to stay here and hold him. Or if that would keep him awake, she'd go and have a cup of tea with Ted and then creep back after Hugo fell asleep and sit in the chair next to his bed.

'If I'm going to be here for the next twenty-four hours, I need someone to fill in for me at the meeting tomorrow afternoon. I thought you might do it.'

'Me? But I can't!'

'Why not? You know all the issues, and I think that the clinic means as much to you as it does to me.'

'Yes, it does. But it's *you* they want to see. We can put it off…'

'That's not going to be so easy, the arrangements have already been made. And you'll be speaking directly for me.' He moved his left arm stiffly, catching her hand, his thumb moving across the ring on her finger. 'That gives you the right.'

'That's just a pretence, Hugo.'

'You want the same things I do. I trust you to speak for me. That's not a pretence.'

'Is it what you really want?'

'Yes, it is. Isn't it what you'd want?'

In his place, she'd do exactly the same. She'd want Hugo out there, working for the thing that was most important to her, instead of cooling his heels, drinking tea at the hospital. Even if the prospect of going to the meeting alone was terrifying, Hugo seemed to think that she could do it.

'Okay. I'll stay a little longer…'

'No, you'll go now and get some sleep. Ted will take you to the meeting, and he'll point you in the right direction, who to greet first and so on. You'll knock them dead.'

'You really think so?'

'Yes, I do. Go. Although if you could get me a phone first, I want to call my father.'

'I'll find Ted, you can use his.'

'Thanks.'

Nell climbed off the bed, pulling her dress straight. It seemed to have survived the evening tolerably well, which was a tribute to its quality. She fussed with it, aware that she was putting off the moment of leaving.

'I'll…call you. In the morning.' She picked up her clutch bag, checking unnecessarily that the diamond necklace and bracelet, which she'd finally managed to take off in the car on the way to hospital, were still safely inside.

'Wait…' Hugo was grinning now. 'You were thinking

of leaving without kissing me goodbye? Just on the cheek, I don't want the monitor to register anything that gives my doctor pause for thought.'

Nell laughed, bending over him. 'First you tell me how you really feel.'

'Dreadful. I ache in muscles I never knew I had.'

'Good. You'll be well cared for here, and I'll be back tomorrow, after the meeting. Think you can be awake for me?'

'I'll do my very best.' Hugo pulled her down for a kiss that set Nell's heart thumping. Goodness only knew what was going on with the monitor, and she didn't dare look. 'Go. Before I decide I'm feeling a lot better now and I need another one of those…'

Having Nell walk away had been more difficult than he'd thought. Hugo kept it together until Ted had come and then gone again, and then there was nothing to prevent his thoughts from ranging wherever they wanted to go. However much he craved having her with him now, this was what he wanted her to do. He wanted Nell to walk out of that meeting tomorrow feeling the exhilaration of having taken it by storm. She'd been bullied and made to feel ashamed for much too long.

Maybe if he'd done the same with Anna, given her some way of taking her own career forward while she was with him, then things might have been different. But he doubted it. Anna had told him that she lived in his shadow even when he wasn't there, and that she couldn't handle it. Things were working with Nell because, despite what everyone thought, they weren't in love. He should remember that, just in case he felt any temptation to fall in love with her.

It wouldn't be all that hard. She was beautiful and brave, and when she was there he forgot all about whether or not his heart would keep beating. He knew that it would, just so he'd be able to spend another moment with her. But if he fell in love, things would change. However hard he tried, Nell's career would have to take second place to the duties that he'd been born to.

His limbs felt heavy, and he could hardly keep his eyes open. Hugo realised that the tablet he'd taken from the nurse, not even thinking to question what it was, was probably a sleeping pill. As he drifted into sleep, he wondered briefly what it might be like to fall asleep with Nell at his side.

Nell had called him before going into the lunch meeting, her nerves jangling in the cadence of her voice. When she called him again, a little more than two hours later, she sounded quite different.

'I did the presentation, just the way you did last time. They really liked it, Hugo.'

'I'm sure they did.' Hugo leaned back against the pillows, smiling.

'They're going to help us.'

Hugo grinned. 'It didn't occur to me for one moment that they wouldn't.'

'Well, it occurred to me. I thought they might chase me away and say that they'd come to hear you, and I just wasn't good enough.'

'When are you going to realise that you're always good enough, Nell?'

There was a pause, and Hugo imagined Nell frowning, the way she did whenever he complimented her.

'I'm not sure how you can say "always" good enough. There are a lot of things you haven't seen me do yet. But I was good enough today.'

That was something. If large oaks could grow from little acorns, then one of these days Nell was going to stand up and command the attention she deserved. Until then, Hugo would just keep pushing, one inch at a time.

'Did your parents come to see you?'

'My father did. Mother obviously decided that it was safe to allow us in the same room unsupervised.'

'And was it?'

'We disagreed on a few things. Patched it up again. We're good.' Better than they had been for a very long time. Hugo wondered whether Nell knew that it was her influence that had made that possible.

'Are you getting out this afternoon?'

'Yes. I've been pronounced none the worse for wear and I can go as soon as you can collect me.'

Nell laughed, the sound of pure happiness reaching him despite the less-than-perfect phone connection.

'That's great. We're on our way now.'

She almost danced into his room a little later. Nell was wearing a red summer jacket over a red-and-white printed dress, and Hugo began to wish that he'd been with her at the luncheon. But then she would have sat quietly beside him, supporting him but hardly speaking up for herself. She could do so much more than that.

'Are you ready? Before we go, I have someone who'd like to see you.'

Hugo just wanted to go down to the car and get home. But then Nell ducked outside the doorway, appearing again with a wheelchair.

'Uncle Hugo!' Nadine beamed at him.

'Nadine. What are you doing here?'

'I came to see you, silly.' Nadine wrinkled her nose at him and he laughed.

'That's very kind of you. Who told you that I was here?'

'Dr Nell. She said you were ill but you're better now.'

'Yes, that's right.' Nell pulled up a chair and Hugo sat

down, facing the wheelchair and leaning forward towards Nadine.

'Are you *all* better?'

'Yes, every bit of me. And what about you? You look much better than when I saw you last.'

Nadine nodded. 'Mama and Papa are taking me home soon.'

'That's good news.' Hugo flipped his gaze up towards Nell, and she nodded, smiling. Clearly she'd taken a moment to find out how Nadine was, and the little girl was recovering well.

'Were you lonely?' Nadine looked around the room that Hugo had occupied. He supposed that the exaggerated quiet of the private wing of the hospital must seem a little lonely to her.

'Yes, I was a bit lonely. But I was only here for one day.'

Nadine nodded, tugging at the teddy bear that was squashed down beside her in the wheelchair. A little tatered now, Claude had accompanied Nadine through most of her stays at the hospital. When she stretched out her hands, offering him to Hugo, he felt his eyes fill with tears.

'Are we going to see how Claude is?' How many times had he pressed his stethoscope to Claude's chest to dispel a little girl's fears? He knew something about those fears now, the unspoken shadows that defied everything he'd learned as a doctor.

'How *you* are.' Nadine was growing up. She knew that Claude was just a way of talking about her own difficulties, and she was offering him to Hugo in the hope that he might speak for him, too. Hugo's hand automatically reached for the stethoscope that wasn't in his pocket, and decided instead to just press his ear to Claude's chest.

'I hear it...' He nodded, hearing only the pounding of his own heart. 'That's very good...'

'Perfect.' Nadine echoed the word he usually said when

he listened to Claude's heart. It had been on the tip of Hugo's tongue but somehow he'd been unable to say it in connection with himself. Hugo nodded, giving Claude a hug and then passing him back to Nadine.

'It's time to go back now, Nadine.' Nell spoke in her careful, studied French, but the warmth of her smile was unmistakable. 'Your mother will be here to see you.'

Hugo couldn't let her go yet. This little girl who had been through so much but had still found it in her to offer him the comfort of a teddy bear. 'Would you like me to come with you?'

Nadine nodded, and Nell flashed him a querying glance. Hugo realised that his jeans and casual shirt weren't his usual attire for the hospital, but that didn't seem to matter right now. He got to his feet, releasing the brakes on the wheelchair.

Hugo had breezed past the nurses, smiling as he went but not stopping to receive his printed discharge papers. Nell had collected them for him, and followed him through the building to the children's section of the cardiac unit. A couple of the staff obviously noticed that he was dressed particularly casually today and might have wondered, but Hugo didn't seem to care and neither did any of the children in the ward. Nadine was settled comfortably back into her bed, and Hugo spent time talking and playing with her and all the other children.

He seemed to light up when he was around them. After an hour, it still didn't seem that Hugo was about to leave and Nell stepped in, dragging him away. He'd had enough for one day and there was no question about whether Hugo would be back soon, despite the fact that he was still on leave of absence from the hospital and had so very recently been one of its patients.

'They've been through so much. I feel like a complete

fraud.' He murmured the words as he got into the back seat of the car, next to Nell.

'You need to stay strong, Hugo. Who's going to champion them if you don't?' This afternoon had brought exactly what she and Hugo were doing into sharp perspective. If the endless meeting and lunches had seemed less important than being on the wards, it would make a huge difference to both the patients and the doctors and nurses who worked here.

He laughed suddenly, taking her hand, even though no one was looking. 'And who's going to champion *me* if you don't?'

'I expect you'll find someone.' Every time he got too close, she instinctively drew back. Then kicked herself for it, because being close to Hugo was the best thing that she could imagine.

The car slowed a little and Hugo nudged her. On the pavement a couple of women were waving at them, and Hugo waved back.

'Wave…' he murmured to Nell.

'They're not interested in me.'

'No?' He turned to her in disbelief. 'Try waving and see what happens.'

Ted had obligingly bought the car almost to a halt. Nell leaned across and waved at the women, feeling rather stupid, but they reacted by waving even more enthusiastically. A small boy standing next to them on the pavement started to jump up and down, catching their excitement.

Hugo caught her hand up, pressing it to his lips, and the women laughed, nudging each other. Ted waited a few more seconds and then applied his foot to the accelerator.

'That's nice of them.' Nell watched through the back window as the car moved away.

Hugo nodded. If only the women knew that this was

all a sham. Nell sat back in her seat, suddenly feeling dispirited.

'By the way, I've postponed my meeting for tomorrow. We can fit it in next week.' Perhaps he felt the same. Hugo seemed keen to change the subject.

'Are you sure you're feeling all right?'

'I feel fine. But another day's rest couldn't hurt.'

Nell had assumed that as soon as Hugo got out of hospital he'd be as unstoppable as the last time. 'Have you got something up your sleeve, Hugo? You're not going to tell me you're going paragliding or something?'

'No. Seems you've got me under control…'

Nell snorted with laughter. 'Right. That's never going to happen, Hugo.'

CHAPTER THIRTEEN

HUGO HAD TO admit that these few days' rest had done him good. He felt stronger, less fearful, and less of a slave to the imagined beat of his heart.

But now it was time to get back to work, and Nell accompanied him to a presentation to the board of directors in the most prestigious of the few high-rise offices in Montarino. It was one of their most important meetings so far, and Nell seemed to dwindle into the background, hanging on to his arm and supporting him. It wasn't until he'd got up to speak that the idea in Hugo's head became a reality.

He thanked everyone for being there, and reiterated the importance of the project that they were being asked to help sponsor. Then he introduced Nell, and sat down.

She kicked him so hard under the table that he jumped. But she got to her feet, smiling. She made a charming apology for any shortcomings in her French, making a joke about having to learn so that she knew what her fiancé was up to. Everyone laughed, and then the lights went down and the first of the images from Hugo's laptop appeared, projected onto the wall. She then proceeded to make a presentation of such vigour and freshness that even Hugo felt he would have given anything that she asked of him.

She waited until they were in the car again before she turned on him. Hugo shifted his feet away from her, just in case she decided to kick him again.

'What are you doing, Hugo?'

'I'm doing the best I can for the clinic. You had them eating out of your hand.'

'You!' She pointed at him accusingly. 'They wanted you, not me.'

'Maybe they went in wanting me. Unless I'm very much mistaken, by the time you'd finished with them, they'd forgotten about tax deductions and publicity, and they wanted a clinic.'

'You might have told me first.'

'Yes, you made that plain. I'm sorry, I was improvising.'

'Well, don't do it again, Hugo. Next time you *tell* me what you're about to do.'

The pink of her cheeks, Nell's passion, and her unerring sense of how to capture hearts. He'd do anything not to see that subsumed into the quiet, submissive woman who had walked next to him into the building.

'All right. So that means you'll do the next presentation?'

'This is *your* project, Hugo. You're the boss.'

He didn't want to be the boss, in Nell's eyes. He wasn't someone whose opinion of her might drag her down and make her feel any less than she was. But on the other hand, being the boss did give him the opportunity to build her up, and he decided to let go of the question of who was supposed to be telling who to do what.

'So I'm making a decision. You do it better than I can.' He leaned forward, hoping for some support. 'Don't you think so, Ted?'

Ted was keeping his eye on the road and didn't turn. 'I didn't catch that…'

Right. Ted was keeping out of it. Wise move, probably. But if Hugo was venturing where angels feared to tread, he wasn't going to back down now. It meant far too much to him.

'So you'll do the presentation tomorrow?'

Nell was trying to glare at him, but she couldn't quite conceal her pleasure. 'I'll think about it.'

Hugo closed his eyes, trying to conceal *his* pleasure. Things were going in the right direction.

'Ted… Ted, look…'

'I see it.' The car slowed suddenly, and Hugo opened his eyes. For a moment he remembered the pain from the stun gun, and almost threw his arm protectively across Nell before he realised that they weren't under any threat.

At the side of the road, a car had veered off the road, breaking through a fence that bounded a field. Another car, which had stopped at the side of the road, was crushed at the front right-hand side and a young man was climbing slowly out of it.

Almost before Ted had brought the car to a halt, Nell had the door on her side open and was climbing out. Wobbling a little on her high heels, she ran over to the man, calling to him and then changing direction, making for the car that was in the ditch.

'We're going to need the first aid kit, Ted.' Hugo climbed out of the car, knowing that Ted would follow him with the medical kit they carried in the boot. He ran over to where Nell was sliding precariously down a grassy slope towards the stricken car.

This time, he supported her. Reaching out with his right hand, he grabbed her elbow to stop her from falling as they both hurried towards the car. As they approached, Hugo could hear the sound of a baby crying.

Nell carefully pulled the driver's door of the car open. A woman was sitting inside, trapped by the crushed dashboard and steering column. Mercifully, it seemed that she was just unconscious.

'I'll take her.' Hugo knelt down on the grass, reaching in with his good arm to find a pulse. 'You get the baby out.'

'Right.' Nell opened the back door of the car, reaching in towards the baby carrier in the back seat. It was still firmly strapped in, and that seemed to have saved the child from any injury if the noise it was making was anything to go by. But the angle of the car made it awkward to get to.

She crawled inside without a moment's hesitation. Hugo felt a flash of regret, wanting to be the one to go inside the car but knowing that Nell was the better choice right now. He bit back his feelings, turning quickly to the woman in the front seat.

Behind him, he could hear Ted calling for an ambulance and a fire and rescue truck. Then another voice came to his ears.

'Is she all right?'

The man from the other car was standing right behind him, blood beginning to trickle down the side of his face. Ted ended his call and stepped forward, ushering him away. He would check him over for any signs of serious injury, and with the information that Hugo had now, he had to concentrate on the woman. He could see blood beginning to pool under the seat but couldn't see where it was coming from. She was pinned down by the infrastructure of the car, and even if she hadn't been, Hugo was loath to move her until the ambulance arrived with the proper equipment.

The woman was breathing but still unconscious. Carefully he pushed his fingers between the seat and her legs, but there was no blood there. The bleeding must have been further down, and he couldn't see her lower legs. Quickly checking her chest and stomach, Hugo turned his attention to craning inside, cursing quietly as he felt his left shoulder pull. There was no time to think about that right now.

* * *

Nell climbed inside the car, sliding across to where the baby was secured on the back seat. Fumbling with the nylon mesh straps, she found that one of them had become caught when the front passenger seat had been forced back a few inches in the crash.

But it seemed that the baby was unhurt. Quickly she crawled backwards out of the car, opening the medical kit that Ted had brought and searching for a scalpel. It registered at the back of her mind that as car medical kits went, this one was particularly well-stocked and it looked as if Hugo might need it. The woman in the front seat of the car still wasn't moving.

She climbed back inside the car, cutting the straps around the car seat with the scalpel and carefully pulling the car seat free. Laying it down on the grass, she examined the baby for any signs of injury.

'Okay?' Ted's voice behind her sounded as if he was fighting with a lump in his throat.

'Yes, I can't see any injuries at all.' The baby was still screaming, tears squeezing their way down its crumpled little face, and Nell tried vainly to comfort it. 'How's the driver of the other car?'

'Okay. Cut on his head. Someone else has stopped and they're sitting with him.'

'Right. Let me know if things change. Can you…um… do anything…?' She gestured towards the carrier. If the baby and the other driver were all right, she should help Hugo.

'Yep.' Ted leaned over the car seat, his thick fingers suddenly tender as he smoothed the child's head then brushed his finger against the palm of its hand. It opened its eyes, still grizzling fitfully.

'Great. Nice one.' Nell assumed the manoeuvre wasn't in any royal bodyguard's manual, so it must be in the one that came with being a father of three girls. Ted nodded, picking up the seat and carrying it over to their car.

'How is she?' Hugo was bending down awkwardly, trying to see into the footwell of the car.

'Airways are clear, and I can see no signs of internal bleeding. She's injured somewhere, though, and I think it's her lower legs.'

'Let me see.' Nell pressed her lips together. Implying that he couldn't do his job was a bitter pill for Hugo to swallow, but right now their feelings didn't matter. They had to make the right decisions for the woman in the car.

Hugo stepped back immediately. 'Can you see anything?'

'No, not from this side. I'll see if I can get to her from the passenger seat.' Nell straightened up and started to walk around the car. Hugo couldn't do this. He was bigger than she was, and although his shoulder was improving, it still hampered his movement.

'Be careful…' He shot her an admonishing glance and Nell nodded.

It was a struggle to get the passenger door open, but she managed it. Climbing inside, she bent down, trying to see through the twisted metal.

'I can see her legs. She's pinned but…yes, I can see where the blood's coming from.' Nell stretched out, gripping the woman's leg just below the knee, and the blood that was coming from a large gash on her lower leg began to ooze slower.

'Can you reach the wound?'

'Just about. Pass me some dressings, would you? I think I can pack a temporary dressing around it, just to stop the bleeding a bit, until they get her out.'

Hugo leaned in to pass the dressings to her. 'Give me the ring. If you get it caught on something…'

'Yes. Thanks.' Nell had seen de-gloved fingers, where

rings had been caught in machinery, during her stint in A & E, when she'd been training. She pulled the bulky ring off and put it into Hugo's hand. 'How's she doing?'

'Vital signs seem steady.'

Nell wriggled forward, leaning down to apply the dressings to the woman's wound. It was awkward work in the confined space, and she ended up half on the seat and half lying in the footwell. As she finished, she saw the woman's foot twitch.

'She's moving, Hugo. Might be coming round…' Hugo would need to try and keep her still, and that wasn't going to be easy.

'Okay. I've got her.'

Nell heard the woman moan, and what sounded like an attempt at words. Hugo's arm across her legs was keeping her relatively still, and he was talking to her, replying to her incoherent cries.

'Your baby's safe and well. I'm a doctor and we'll have you out of here soon. Try to stay still for me.'

The woman's leg moved a little and she screamed in pain. Hugo quieted her and Nell heard the sound of weeping.

'All right, sweetheart. Hold on to me.'

A siren, which cut off abruptly, heralded the arrival of the ambulance. Then voices, telling Hugo to move back, which changed their tone considerably when he turned around and the ambulance crew recognised him. He updated them on the woman's condition and asked what analgesics they carried with them. After some conversation he turned back to Nell.

'I'm giving her a shot of morphine. Are you all right down there?'

'Yep.' Nell's back was twisted uncomfortably and her arm was beginning to ache. But she didn't dare move in case the dressings were dislodged and the woman started bleeding again.

After what seemed like an age, but was probably only a few minutes, Nell heard another siren. She heard Hugo talking to someone and squeezed her eyes closed, concentrating on holding the dressings in place and ignoring the ache in her back. Hugo would take care of things. He would deal with it, and the woman would be brought safely out of the car.

'Okay... Nell, are you still with us?'

'Yep.'

'Good job. They've decided to take the roof of the car off.'

'Right.' Nell had expected that. It made it easier and safer to move someone who might have a spinal injury. And the Jaws of Life should make short work of the car's structure and allow the rescuers to peel the car roof off.

'It looks as if once that's done, they'll be able to free her legs easily. Shouldn't take too long.'

'Good. That'll be good.'

'Tuck your legs in a bit. They'll be using a shield to protect you both from the broken glass.'

Nell moved her legs, tucking them under her as well as she could manage, without letting go of the dressings.

'That's great. Hang on in there, honey.'

Nell felt the car move slightly as it was propped and steadied. Then the sound of the mechanised cutters and the breaking of glass. She concentrated on the woman's leg. It looked as if it needed attention soon.

Hang on in there, honey.

Hugo was always kind and encouraging towards his patients. And perhaps he was, even now, keeping up appearances—she was supposed to be his fiancée. But there was a note in his voice that no one could counterfeit.

The words were just for her, no one else. She repeated

them over and over in her head as she felt the rough brush of a gloved hand against her ankle, moving her leg a little in the constricted space and sending showers of pins and needles down it.

Sunlight filtered down into the footwell as the rescuers peeled the roof off. Then Hugo leaned into the car, his gloved hand over hers, taking over the pressure that she was keeping on the wound.

'Got to stop meeting like this.' His grin and the murmured words were for her too, despite the quiet, concentrated work going on around them.

'Have you got it?' Nell slipped her hand out from under his, and he nodded, his gaze flipping up to somewhere above and behind her.

'Okay, someone's going to help you out now.'

Someone gripped her waist firmly, pulling her backwards. Her leg muscles began to cramp painfully and she grimaced, trying not to cry out as she was hauled out of the car.

'Ça va?' A tall fireman was looking down at her as she sat on the grass, rubbing her leg.

'Oui.' Nell pulled her rumpled skirt down. Not all that demure for a wannabe princess, but as a member of the team who'd just spent the last fifteen minutes in an awkward, half upside-down pose, flashing a little leg could be forgiven. She wondered briefly which one the fireman saw her as.

The latter, clearly. He turned away, leaving her to it, and got on with his job. Nell watched as Hugo and the paramedics quickly ascertained the woman's condition a little better, and Hugo gave the signal for the fire and rescue team to remove the twisted metal that was holding her legs down.

As soon as Nell could stand, she hobbled out of their way and sat back down on the grass, watching. It was a quiet, professional operation, everyone updating everyone else on what was happening, the woman in the car the centre of their attention. The paramedics backed off, leaving Hugo with the woman, as the fire and rescue team made the last, careful removal of pieces from the car. Then they closed in again, carefully lifting the woman from the car and securing her onto a stretcher.

Hugo was still directing operations, speaking briefly to Ted, who climbed into the ambulance with the baby, still in its car seat. Hugo followed him, obviously intent on a last examination of the woman and her child, to make sure that they were ready for the journey to the hospital. Nell sat alone and unnoticed, watching the fire and rescue team pack up their equipment.

Then Hugo climbed down from the back of the ambulance and the driver shut the doors. He walked across the grass towards her and sat down stiffly.

'How is she?' Nell looked up at him, knowing that the answer would be written on his face.

'Her legs are broken and she's lost a lot of blood. No sign of spinal injury, and although she's drifting in and out of consciousness, which is a worry, I don't see any head trauma either. They'll do a CAT scan...' He lapsed into silence, realising perhaps that his face had already told Nell what she wanted to know. There was every reason to be optimistic.

'Good. And you're okay?'

'Yes. I knew there was a reason for the last couple of days' rest.' He chuckled, and then saw Nell's hand, still absent-mindedly rubbing her leg. 'Cramp?'

'Yes. It just aches a bit now. Ted's going with them?'

Hugo grinned. 'He's going to see that the baby's all right and handed over to its family.'

'Good.' Nell chuckled. 'Think he'll give it up that easily?'

'They might have a bit of a struggle on their hands. He's bonding fast.'

They sat together in silence as the ambulance drew away, followed by the fire and rescue truck. The other driver was standing by a police car that had arrived at the scene and was parked a couple of hundred yards along the carriageway, and the people who had stopped had got back into their cars and resumed their journeys.

It was suddenly quiet. In between the swoosh of passing vehicles, Nell could hear birds singing and the sun was warm on her face. If it hadn't been for her own crumpled dress and the spots of blood on the rolled-up sleeves of Hugo's white shirt, it would have been a fine day for a walk in the countryside.

'Have you seen my shoes?' A thought struck her.

'Ted put them in the car.' Hugo turned his face up to the sun, as if he were thinking the very same thing. It was the quiet after a storm, in which they both began to move from the urgency of a wrecked car by the roadside back into the other reality of their everyday lives.

Or back into Hugo's reality. However much he tried to involve her, it seemed as if he was just giving her something to do, making her feel as if she wasn't just an accessory on his arm. But in truth, that's what she was. This was Hugo's country, and his mission, and Nell was just helping him out for a while. She'd be back in London, reading about him in the newspapers, before very long.

'Why so glum?' Nell turned to find that he was looking steadily at her.

'Nothing. I was just hoping that the woman will be all right.' She got to her feet, flexing the still-sore muscles in her leg, watching as Hugo stood. He was holding his left arm loosely by his side, not moving it but seeming to have suffered no ill effects from his exertions.

He opened the back door of his car, motioning her inside, and Nell stood her ground. 'If you think you're going to drive...'

'No, I don't think that.' He reached into his pocket, drawing out the car keys and put them into her hand. 'Just get into the back for a moment.'

Nell got in, shifting over to let him follow her. He closed the door and then turned, reaching for her ankle and propping her leg up onto his lap. 'Looks as if your leg's still sore, which gives me a marvellous opportunity to return the favour you've been doing me.'

The look in his eyes wasn't anything like Nell hoped that her demeanour was when she massaged his shoulder. But his face was the model of propriety. She sat still, feeling his fingers on the back of her leg, just above the knee.

'Ah!' For a moment, all she could think about was his touch. And the way that the sore muscle at the back of her leg was reacting and then relaxing as his fingers pressed a little harder. 'That's it. A bit higher?'

It sounded a little bit like sex, and felt a lot like it, too. Rather than stare into his eyes, the way that she wanted to, she squeezed them shut.

'Right there?' Even his voice sounded like the honey-smooth tones of a lover.

'Yes, you've got it. That's much better.'

Her leg felt a great deal better. The rest of her body was beginning to ache for the same touch. Very slow, and as sure as the careful progress of his fingers on her leg. Closing her eyes hadn't been such a good idea after all, she could practically see Hugo making love to her behind her eyelids.

'Thanks. That's fine now.' When she opened her eyes, she thought that she saw the hint of a smile on his face. The dark echoes of what she'd been imagining in his green eyes.

'Wouldn't want your foot to slip off the clutch...' His fingers kept massaging.

'This is an automatic.'

'Ah, yes. Silly me.' Hugo let her go and Nell pushed her skirt back down to her knees. Feeling in his pocket, he brought out the ring. 'Don't forget this.'

Nell smiled, holding out her hand. Whenever she took the ring off, he always put it back on her finger again. She liked that, even if it was only temporary and didn't mean what everyone thought it did.

He leaned towards her, as if he were about to kiss her. But something attracted his attention and Nell turned to see one of the policemen strolling towards the car. Hugo grinned at her, getting out of the car and walking towards the man.

He seemed to have a sixth sense about that. Hugo was always on guard, aware of who was around him and what they were doing. Nell supposed that came from living his life in the spotlight, never being able to walk down the street alone and unnoticed. It was why he guarded his secrets so carefully. He had to know that something was private.

He exchanged a few words with the policeman and Nell climbed into the driver's seat of the car, pulling the seat forward. In the rear-view mirror, she could see him walking back towards her. Relaxed, stains on the knees of his trousers from having bent down beside the injured woman, but still handsome. Still so perfect that Nell could hardly bear it.

She started the car, waiting for him to get in beside her. It was time to get back on the road.

CHAPTER FOURTEEN

HUGO COULD FEEL his strength returning. The bruises were long gone, and the red gash on his chest had knitted well. It would heal into a fine white line, as barely noticeable as the slight change in the contour of the skin above the pacemaker. It was there but rapidly becoming hidden.

He needed Nell less and less each day. He could make his way through a press of people now, without wanting to shy away from them and protect his shoulder. He'd be able to drive in another few weeks, and the exercises that he did every morning, to prevent his shoulder from freezing, could become a little more strenuous.

Nell had thrown herself into raising money for the clinic, and they'd decided that, working apart, they could cover twice as much ground as working together. Hugo missed having her with him, but he knew she enjoyed it, and as time passed, her confidence seemed to be growing.

The best part of the day was always the morning. Dressed in a T-shirt and sweatpants, her hair scrunched on the top of her head, and without a scrap of make-up, Nell was the most beautiful woman he'd ever seen. They'd have breakfast together, discussing their respective commitments for the day. Then he'd put a suit and tie on, and Nell would put on a dress and her engagement ring, and they were ready for the day, their public faces firmly in place.

'So...how would you like a day off?' Hugo had been

thinking of broaching the subject for a while and had decided that there wasn't much to lose by doing so. The worst that could possibly happen was that she could say no.

'A day off?' She was sitting in the sun, the breakfast things in front of her on the patio table. One leg was curled up beneath her, and there was a smudge of marmalade on her thumb. Hugo tried not to look as she licked it off.

'Yes. Remember I still owe you a trip on the royal yacht.'

'That was just for show, Hugo.'

'It doesn't mean we can't go. Take a weekend off, we've both earned it.'

'Isn't there…? Don't you want to spend the time somewhere else?'

Nowhere in the world that he could think of. 'We're supposed to be engaged. I wouldn't dream of spending a weekend anywhere other than with you. And I paid enough for the pleasure of your company.'

Hugo winced. He hadn't meant that quite the way it had sounded and from the look on Nell's face, the joke had fallen flat. It had been a long time since he'd been this tongue-tied when asking a girl out.

'We're not really engaged, remember,' she said quietly.

'I can still enjoy spending time with you, can't I?'

'You don't have to say that here. No one's listening.' There was an edge to Nell's voice now that cut away at Hugo's heart. Suddenly the morning sun seemed harsh and altogether too bright to sit here for any longer.

'Of course. I'm sorry.' He stood up, reaching for his diary, which lay with hers on the table. 'I have an early start this morning. I'll see you this evening.'

She hadn't needed to say it, not like that at least. Nell sat on the patio, wondering whether Hugo would forgive her, and when she heard the front door open and then close, it seemed that he hadn't. She ran to the front window and saw him, immaculate in his suit and tie, getting into the car, while Ted waited at the wheel.

A weekend with Hugo. Sun and the sea, a chance to relax. It had sounded too wonderful to be true.

And in Nell's experience, that usually meant that it was. Beneath all the excitement and glamour, beneath the very real relationship that was growing between them, Hugo was still a prince. He could buy whatever he wanted, and even though there was no contract of employment between them any more, he was as much in control of her future as Martin had been. And she'd allowed that.

She had to get ready. She was due to speak to a women's club at noon, a talk that was designed both to educate them about the signs of heart disease and ask them to spread the word about the plans for the clinic. That was what she was here for, a shared goal and an agreement, which protected his secrets and her reputation. She needed to remember that whenever it started feeling too much that her rightful place was on his arm.

'Nell, I'm so sorry.' Hugo marched into the sitting room, clearly gripped by the urgency of being on a mission. Nell jumped. She hadn't heard him come in.

'You took the words right out of my mouth.' The magazine lying open on her lap had gone unread, while she'd mentally rehearsed her apology.

'I...' He looked suddenly perplexed. Clearly he'd been rehearsing too, and his speech wasn't going entirely to plan. 'You have nothing to apologise for. And since I do, I'm going to break the ladies-first rule.'

'Okay.' When Hugo was in one of these moods, there was no stopping him. Nell had learned to just go with the flow.

He took a breath, as if reorienting himself back on his

trajectory. 'I'm really sorry about this morning. It was just a joke and…all I meant was that money pales into insignificance in the face of the pleasure I'd take in spending a weekend away with you. You owe me nothing, and there's no obligation on your part to join me.'

'I know. It's all right, Hugo, I never thought that was the case. I was just being a bit over-sensitive.'

'No, you weren't. I know you have good reason not to mix business with pleasure, and any implication that I—'

'Please stop, Hugo. Let's just say we're okay, shall we?'

He nodded, bringing out a glossy paper carrier bag from behind his briefcase. 'I was going to bring you flowers but decided on this instead.'

What was this? The carrier bag looked as if it had come from an exclusive store somewhere, and when Hugo handed it to her, Nell saw an embellished cardboard box inside. Too big for jewellery and too heavy for underwear. But in this situation, they'd be gifts that an unsubtle man would bring, and Hugo was never that.

She took the lid off the box and smiled. Perfect. 'Chocolate! Thank you, Hugo.'

He grinned, finally taking his jacket off and sitting down. Nell proffered the box. 'Would you like one?'

'You first.'

The chocolate was delicious, with a centre of dark brandy truffle. 'Mmm…these are gorgeous. You should try one.'

'Thanks… One can't hurt, right?'

'No. One can't hurt.' Even though he had no problem with cholesterol, Hugo's diet was strictly balanced and healthy. Perhaps too much so. Nell had never seen him eat sweets or sugary foods, even as a treat.

Hugo loosened his tie, leaning back on the sofa, taking a moment to appreciate the forbidden chocolate. 'That's good.'

They were friends again. Clearly Hugo didn't care about receiving any apology from Nell, but she cared about giving it.

'Hugo, I'm sorry, too. I didn't mean to infer that you were being in any way insincere. This is just…a difficult situation. I don't know quite how to act sometimes.'

'You're doing just fine. You should never apologise to me, because it's my weakness that's put you into a difficult situation.'

That assumption, again, that he was somehow flawed. Hugo seemed to take it for granted, as if it were beyond argument, and a given thing.

'You're weak because you have a pacemaker? Is that what you say to all your pacemaker patients, that they'll never be the same again?'

'No, of course not…' He broke off, as if the incongruity had only just occurred to him.

'Then why say it to yourself? You know it's not true. Why keep it such a secret?'

He shook his head. 'I don't know, Nell. I feel…different somehow. Less than what I was.'

'But you don't mind relying on a watch to tell you the time. You don't mind relying on your phone to keep you in touch.'

'That's not the same thing. I'm not relying on either of them to keep my heart beating, that's a bit more important.'

'Yes, it's a great deal more important. But what happens if the pacemaker fails? Your heartbeat will probably slow up, but it's not going to stop completely. Most of the time, your heart's beating just fine on its own, the pacemaker only activates when your level of activity increases and you need a little extra help. So the worst that can happen is that you have to stop and sit down. You *know* all this, Hugo.'

'Yes, I do. I…' He looked at her suddenly. 'You're pushing me, aren't you?'

'Yes, I'm pushing you. Because what you know up here...' Nell reached forward, tapping his forehead lightly with her finger '...isn't what you actually feel inside, is it?'

He shrugged. 'No. But I can't change that.'

'You could look at the reasons. Why you blatantly disregard everything your head is telling you.'

'Is this your usual psychology chat?' He narrowed his eyes, and Nell could see that he was only half joking.

'No. This one's just for you.'

Nell had a habit of asking all the questions that Hugo didn't want to answer. He supposed that on some level, he must have known that she'd get around to this sooner or later. Perhaps on some level he'd wanted her to.

'I can't fall short, Nell. I've been given a great deal in life, and it's my duty to repay it.'

'What makes you think you aren't?'

'You've seen the kids at the hospital.' He knew that Nell would understand that.

'Yes, I have. And I know you're doing your best for them. We can't do any more than our best.'

'And my best may not be good enough.' Hugo's greatest fear was right there, on his lips. As if somehow Nell had managed to entrance it, and coax it from its hiding place.

'It's all we have. And we're allowed to take some time out and have a life, to have holidays and take some time off when we're sick.' Nell frowned, and Hugo braced himself for whatever was to follow. He knew that look.

'I can't believe that you don't have someone to come home to at night. That you're so sure you won't that you can commit yourself to a fake engagement for the next few months.'

Hugo had got used to coming home to Nell at night, and it was almost a shock to be reminded that it wasn't real. But he'd made that decision a long time ago.

'That's not as easy as you think, Nell.'

'It's never as easy as anyone thinks. I know that.'

Suddenly he wanted to explain. It was the first time that he'd felt that someone might understand, as a friend.

'I did have someone once. I was going to get married. Anna and I met at medical school in London, and we lived together for a couple of years. I told her that I wanted to come back to Montarino and she wanted to come with me, but when we got here…'

Nell nodded him on.

'I had a new job and got caught up in that and the round of engagements that the palace had planned for me. I was happy to be home and…I didn't look closely enough at what was going on within our relationship. I didn't see that Anna was feeling trapped on the sidelines.'

'She didn't have a job?'

'Everyone expected that she was going to be a royal bride. She was offered a lot of roles as patron of various medical facilities, which would take effect after our marriage, but she didn't want her success to come through me. Anna was worth a great deal more than that, and leaving me and going back to London was the best decision she ever made. She has a fulfilling career now, and a husband who doesn't take up so much space that she can't breathe.'

'It seems a bit unfair to give yourself all the blame.'

'I knew what my life was going to be like, I should have seen that it wouldn't be enough for Anna to live through me. I could have followed her back to London but I didn't, because I felt it was my duty to give whatever I could back to Montarino. That's what I have now, and I feel I'm failing.'

'You're not failing, Hugo. You're just recovering from an operation.'

Hugo looked for the understanding he craved, and found it in her eyes. Suddenly it was too much to bear and he got to his feet. 'Is that our chat done, then? I'll go and make dinner...'

'No, it's not done. I'm not finished with you yet.' She called the words after him, but there was humour in Nell's tone. Maybe she knew that the burden of his duty was feeling a little heavy at the moment.

'What are you going to do?' He chuckled, turning on the tap to wash his hands. 'Find me someone who doesn't mind trailing around after me and playing princess?'

'Are there women like that?' Nell professed just the right amount of surprise, before turning her attention to the box of chocolates. He wanted to walk back into the sitting room and hug her, but right now it was probably better to keep his distance.

'Plenty of them.'

'That sounds a bit boring.'

And that was it, in a nutshell. A career woman, someone like Nell, would always want their own life, free of the constraints of his life. Women who wanted him just because he was a prince generally weren't that interesting after the first couple of dates.

It was a catch-22 situation that held him in limbo. There was no way out that Hugo could see, and he suspected that Nell couldn't either. If she could, she would have mentioned it.

The invitation to spend a weekend on the royal yacht had been given again, and this time Nell had accepted it straight away. If his admission that he felt no woman would want the life he offered her was horribly sad, it also neatly let Nell off the hook. There were no expectations from him, and she could match that by allowing no expectations to infiltrate her own thinking.

They set off early. As they crossed the border into France, the sun came out and Hugo retracted the roof of his convertible. A warm breeze and a handsome prince beside her.

As they approached the motorway, Nell took over the driving, and Hugo lounged in the front seat of the car, enjoying the journey. Dressed in a pair of shorts and a sweatshirt, his short hair ruffled in the breeze, he seemed to finally be getting it into his head that they were on holiday.

It was almost midday when they reached the small, bustling French port where the yacht was moored. Hugo took his place at the wheel again, negotiating the narrow streets of the old town, before driving along the quayside and into the marina.

He drew up alongside a young man in pristine white shorts, with the name of Montarino's royal yacht sewn across the sleeve of his white shirt. He stepped forward, opening the passenger door of the car before Nell could reach for the handle.

Hugo gave him an affable grin. 'Thank you, Louis. How are you?'

'Well, Your Highness. It's good to see you.'

Hugo got out of the car, taking a draught of sea air into his lungs, as if it felt easier to breathe here. 'It's very good to be back. How are your studies going?'

'I've just been sitting my exams. They went well, I think.'

Hugo nodded, tossing the car keys to Louis. 'Let me know when you get your results.'

'Will do, Your Highness.' Louis got into the car, driving it towards the car park, leaving Nell and Hugo standing on the quayside.

'Which one is it?' Nell surveyed the boats moored around the marina. Smaller yachts were tied up against the piers, which extended out into the water, and larger ones were anchored further out.

'That one.' Hugo pointed towards one of the yachts.

It wasn't the largest of the boats there, but it seemed the most elegant, glistening white, and bobbing gracefully on an azure sea.

'It's beautiful. How do we get to it?'

He grinned. 'This way.'

Another man in the same uniform as Louis's helped her down into a motor launch. She looked around for her luggage, but it didn't seem that they were going to be waiting for that. As soon as Hugo was on board, the engine was started and they began to speed way from the land.

'This is wonderful.' Hugo's arm was slung across the back of the seat and she had to move a little closer to him, so that he could hear her over the noise of the engine. 'I already feel spoiled.'

'That's exactly how you're meant to feel.' Hugo's lips brushed against her ear.

She was helped up a set of steps onto the deck of the yacht, Hugo following. Waiting for her was a man who bore the word 'Captain' on the sleeve of his shirt.

'Welcome, Dr Maitland.' He stepped forward, holding out his hand. 'I'm Captain Masson.'

'Thank you.' Nell shook his hand, looking around her. The yacht looked just as white and gleaming close up as it had from the land. 'This is a beautiful vessel.'

'Thank you, ma'am.' Captain Masson beamed at her. 'Where would you like to go?'

Nell turned to Hugo and he shrugged. 'Your call. We can dock somewhere for a little shopping. Or if you prefer swimming there are some nice places to stop off.'

Nell thought for a moment. It seemed a little bit of a waste to spend time shopping and swimming when she could enjoy being here on the yacht. 'The sea. I'd like to go…somewhere on the sea if that's all right?'

'A short trip along the coast perhaps, ma'am?'

'Yes, I'd like that.' Nell glanced at Hugo, wondering if that was what he'd had in mind.

'That's an excellent idea. Thank you, Captain Masson.' Hugo smiled.

'Very well. We'll be on our way very soon, we just have to wait for your luggage. In the meantime, drinks have been laid out on the main deck.'

The captain gestured to his right, and Nell took a couple of uncertain steps in that direction. She felt Hugo take her arm and followed his lead, walking towards a short flight of stairs that led up onto a deck, shaded by awnings and dappled by the sun.

'It's…very formal here.'

Hugo nodded. 'This is the royal yacht, my parents bring important visitors here. The crew don't call the captain by his first name, and neither should I. When we're at sea, his word is law, and it's his responsibility to keep us in one piece if we run into a squall.'

'Are we going to run into a squall?' Nell looked up into the blue, cloudless sky.

'I very much doubt it. Captain Masson will have already looked at the weather forecasts all along the coast, and he'll be counting on giving us a smooth ride. It's just a principle.'

He led her onto the main deck, where a table was set out, with champagne on ice and canapés. Nell ignored the seats arranged around the deck in both the sun and the shade, preferring to lean against the wooden-topped rails to watch as the motor launch sped back towards the land and then returned with Louis and their luggage.

As the muted sound of the engines reached her, and the yacht began to move slowly, Hugo joined her, leaning with his back against the rail. 'What do you think?'

'This is wonderful, Hugo. A real treat, thank you.'

CHAPTER FIFTEEN

HUGO WAS HAPPY. Nell was happy, and shining with excitement as he showed her around the yacht. She expressed surprise at the size of her cabin, insisting on looking through each of the portholes to ascertain whether there was a different view from any of them. She explored all the decks, leaning over the rails to see as much as she could.

When the expected message came from Captain Masson, inviting her to the bridge, she ran after Louis's retreating back, seemingly determined to deliver her acceptance of the invitation herself.

He watched as she asked questions about all the instruments and examined the navigation charts that were brought out for her to see. When she was accorded the singular honour of being allowed to take the helm for a while, Captain Masson talked her through making a small corrective manoeuvre, rather than simply letting her hold the wheel, and Hugo saw the helmsman smile. If they weren't careful, the crew would be renaming the yacht after her.

'I hope I didn't take up too much of Captain Masson's time.' The yacht lurched suddenly and she almost stumbled down the steps from the bridge. Hugo caught her arm to steady her.

'All right?' She'd stopped, clutching the handrail, one hand on her chest.

'Yes...yes, I'm all right. I felt a little bit queasy just

then. It's passed now.' She squinted out towards the horizon. 'Are the waves getting bigger?'

'A little, yes. You'll get used to the motion of the ship soon, but if you feel sick we've got a full stock of medication to choose from.'

'No, thanks. I'm fine now. I think my sea legs are kicking in.'

Hugo nodded, watching her down the remainder of the steps. It was probably best to take her mind off the idea of being sick, and mention to Captain Masson that a smooth ride would be appreciated.

'The captain doesn't let just anyone take the helm, you know.' He took her arm, strolling towards the main deck so that they could sit in the afternoon sun.

Nell's cheeks regained their colour suddenly. 'He's very kind. And it's all so interesting. I wonder if he'd let me watch when we stop for the evening and put the anchor down. I'd keep out of the way.'

'I'd be very surprised if he hasn't already got that in mind.' Nell didn't seem to care much for the prestige of being here, but she loved the yacht and wanted to know everything about it. Captain Masson and his crew had seen that, and Hugo reckoned that the dropping of the anchor would be carried out under Nell's command.

And that was the difference. The one that meant that Nell was beyond his reach. She didn't care to spend her days off in the usual leisure pursuits, she wanted to know how things worked. He'd seen her out in the garden at his house, questioning the gardener about how the mix of planting gave year-round colour and helping him weed. She threw herself into her work with the same gusto. Her life had purpose, a life that should never be squashed by his.

But for today and tomorrow, he had her here with him. That had to be enough, because it was all he dared take from Nell.

* * *

At dusk, they came to anchor outside a coastal town, and Nell watched the lights begin to come on, growing brighter as the sky became darker. Then stars appeared in a sky that looked as if it were putting on a show just for her.

Dinner was in the open air on the main deck. Candles on the table, protected from the warm breeze by glass shades. And Hugo, looking far more handsome than he had any right to, in a white open-necked shirt.

'Tonight's a night for dancing.' They'd had their after-dinner coffee, and all that Nell could think was that he was right. Tonight *was* a night for dancing.

She rose, smiling, wondering where the music would come from. Hugo took her in his arms, humming the snatches of a tune and moving her to its slow rhythm.

Perfect. On a perfect night like this, it seemed quite natural that he should kiss her. When he did, it felt as if she were melting into him. As if together they could be at one with the stars and the breeze and just be, without needing to think about the consequences.

'I wish...' They were still moving, dancing together as they kissed.

'What do you wish? If it's anything that I can grant, it's yours.' He whispered the words, leaving a kiss behind them.

'I wish that there was nothing to stop us.'

He knew what she meant. Every line of his body hinted that this could so easily be a seduction, if they'd only let it.

'Is there anything? What happens at sea might be persuaded to stay at sea.'

'We're not exactly at sea.' Nell clung to the last vestiges of her sanity. Even if stars were dancing in the sky, the lights of land were closer than that.

'We're not on dry land either. We might be able to see them, but they can't see us.'

It was tempting. *Very* tempting. Surely she and Hugo could leave everything behind, just for one night?

'I can't leave myself behind. I brought my baggage with me, and you brought yours.'

'You're right. As always.' He kissed her again, warm and unhurried, as if to show that being right didn't mean that she could escape his tenderness.

'Thank you for a wonderful day, Hugo. And a wonderful evening...' The thought that this wonderful evening might so easily become a wonderful night was tearing at her resolve. Nell broke free of his arms. She had to go now, while she still could.

What...*what*...had he been thinking? Hugo put his head around the galley door to thank the chef for his efforts tonight, and walked to his cabin.

It had seemed so natural. Taking her in his arms, letting the breeze take them with it, away from the land and into a place where only desire mattered. But Nell was always the more sensible of the two of them. He should heed her judgement, and remember that there was no possibility that they could make a future together, however tantalising tonight might be. He sat down on the bed, slowly unbuttoning his shirt.

And there was another thing. Hugo rose, walking into the en suite bathroom, pulling his shirt to one side, as if seeing the scar could finally convince him. However many times Nell told him he wasn't, he still felt flawed. And Nell deserved only the best.

A knock sounded, and he dragged his gaze away from the mirror, closing his shirt before he opened the cabin door. Hugo froze.

'You'll keep me standing here?' Nell smiled up at him. Her hair was still gathered up around her head, stray curls escaping around her face. Her eyes were as bright as the moonlight, as if she'd brought a little of it below deck with her.

'No! Come in.' He stood back from the door and she walked into his cabin. For a moment, all he could think was that her feet were bare, and that she walked as if she were floating on air.

Hugo closed the door behind her and leaned against it, as if somehow that might stop this dream from escaping.

'I came to ask you if you'd like to come to my cabin. We could…see the sunrise tomorrow.'

He reached out and touched the sleeve of the ivory-coloured wrap that covered her body. Even that seemed unbearably erotic, since it was clear that she had little else on.

'I would love to come to your cabin. Although I can take or leave the sunrise.'

She nodded. 'Me, too.'

Suddenly she was in his arms, and Hugo found his strength again. He kissed her, tracing his fingers across the soft, silky fabric of her wrap. It was so thin that he could feel her response, the heat of her skin and the sudden tightening of the muscles of her back. He could do this. He could make her cry out for him.

Wordlessly, he wrapped his arm around her and opened the door, looking out to make sure that no one was in the corridor outside then hurrying her forward to her own cabin door. When they were inside, she turned, twisting the lock. The sharp snap seemed to echo through his senses.

'I'm at your mercy now.' Hugo could feel that his own body was ready for hers, and if it let him down, then he knew she'd be kind. Nell was always kind.

'And I'm at yours…' She began to undo the knot in the sash at her waist, leaving the last twist in place, as an obvious invitation for him to finish the job. Hugo stepped forward, taking her in his arms and pulling the sash open.

It seemed unlikely that Nell could be prey to the same

madness that he was, but he felt it. Her whole body was
trembling, moving against his. When he pulled the wrap
from her shoulders, finding a narrow lace strap underneath, she let out a little gasp and he heard the same need
as he felt.

Moonlight slanted across the bed. He wanted so badly
to be a part of that moonlight, making love to her in its
cool gleam. No sooner had the thought occurred to him
than he felt Nell's hand, bunched in his shirt, pulling him
towards the bed.

His heartbeat seemed to ramp up, leaving him almost
breathless. Suddenly she was still.

'It's okay, Hugo.' She laid her hand on his chest. 'It's
not going to let you down.'

It was Nell who wouldn't let him down. Always knowing, always understanding. He kissed her, feeling the
thump of his heart against hers. And suddenly it didn't
feel like a precursor of doom. It felt good.

'Your heart and mine, Nell. Beating together.'

'That means we're both alive.' She smiled up at him.

'I feel more alive than I have for a long time…'

Hugo sat down on the bed, spreading his legs and pulling her close, kissing the wide strip of flesh between the
open fronts of her robe. He felt her hands on his shoulders,
and heard her cry out when he ran his tongue lightly across
her stomach. He could see now that the robe had concealed
ivory lace underwear, and he felt another jolt of longing.
More time, more pleasure involved in taking that off.

She sank down onto his knee, and he held her close,
kissing her and gently working her free of the wrap. It slid
down, draping around his leg.

'You are so beautiful, Nell.' He heard his own voice,
thick with desire.

'You are, too. I want you to make love to me, Hugo.'

She was working on the last few buttons of his shirt, pulling it from his shoulders.

A stab of self-doubt cut through the desire. It was impossible that she couldn't have felt it, he was hers already in as many ways as he could think of. She ran her fingers lightly over the scar on his chest, and he shivered.

'It'll be okay.' She laid her hand on the side of his face, kissing him on the lips. 'Believe me, Hugo.'

Suddenly he did. He let her pull his shirt off, and as she ran her fingers across his chest, he gave himself up to her caresses.

They were both so aroused already that even the smallest gesture seemed to provoke a reaction. When Hugo brushed his fingers across the lace that covered her breasts, Nell felt a sharp tug of desire. When she laid her hand on his belt buckle, she felt him tremble, as if just the thought, just the implication of an action, was as potent as the deed itself.

Undressing each other slowly was an expression of a shared need, which demanded that they take each moment and make it last. The leisurely rocking motion of the yacht seemed to follow their pace, as unstoppable as the movement of the ocean.

And Hugo was all hers. No more fears, no looking over his shoulder. He took pleasure just as wholeheartedly as he gave it, smiling up at her when she found herself on top of him, astride his hips.

'Doesn't anyone ever call you Penelope?'

'No.' On his lips, her given name seemed to sparkle. 'You like it?'

'Yes, I do.'

'I like hearing you say it.' This was something that she could share, just with him.

He chuckled, pulling her down for a kiss. 'Penelope.' He said it again, gasping it when she lowered her body onto his, taking him inside her. When he gripped her hips, pushing her further towards her own climax, he may have said it. By that time, Nell was a little beyond thought. But he did say it again as she clung to him, turning her over to explore every angle of their lovemaking.

He was her heart. Even that thought didn't seem out of place tonight, because there *was* no tomorrow.

'I loved the lace...' They were sprawled together on the bed, whispering the quiet minutes of the night away. 'Is that what you usually wear?'

Nell grinned. She'd hoped he *would* like it. 'It's my body armour.'

'Really? Can't say it worked too well in that regard.' Hugo kissed the top of her head.

'I noticed. But a good friend always used to say that if you're feeling a little under-confident, nice underwear helps.'

'You've been feeling under-confident?'

'I'm not as used to standing up in front of a lot of people as you are. Or having people notice me on the street, or seeing my face on the front pages of the paper.'

He laughed quietly. 'Okay. So you were wearing lace when you first met me?'

'No, if you remember I was fresh off the plane. I was dressed for comfort.'

'So when we talked, that first time at the palace?'

'Yes.'

He sighed. 'At the luncheon? When you bid for me?'

'Of course. What part of that day did you think wasn't a challenge?'

'If I'd known...' His hand went to his forehead, as if he'd just realised an irrefutable truth. 'Actually, if I'd known I wouldn't have been able to get a word out. Probably best that I didn't.'

'I don't imagine you as ever being lost for words, Hugo.'

He rolled over, covering her body with his. Kissing her, with more than a hint of the desire that had filled them both tonight. 'Maybe you should consider the idea. You leave me speechless.'

Hugo felt whole. Wholly happy, more than wholly satisfied, and…just whole. He hadn't felt that way since he'd first felt the signs that his heart might not be working as well as it should. Nell had somehow seen something different in him, and had never shown any doubt about his ability to recover and lead the life that Hugo had thought he'd lost.

That had been his mistake. He'd wanted to put his illness and his operation behind him so badly that he'd tried to rush it. Hugo saw a lot of things differently now. And one thing that he saw with complete certainty was that tonight wasn't going to be enough.

Nell was sleeping now and Hugo fought the temptation to watch her sleep. If he wanted to keep everything that he'd found, he needed to be strong.

Opening her eyes came with a sudden burst of nausea. The whole cabin seemed to be pitching and rolling, taking her stomach with it. Nell closed her eyes, and then opened them again quickly when the feeling that she might be about to die washed over her.

She wasn't about to die. She was just going to be— No. Not now. Please, not now…

Her stomach wasn't listening. Hand over her mouth, Nell rolled off the bed, half staggering and half crawling to the bathroom. The door banged shut behind her, and the whole world lurched.

'Nell…?'

She heard Hugo's voice, but even that couldn't stop her from being sick. Trembling, she called back to him.

'I'm okay. Go away...' Naked and being sick in the bathroom wasn't the best way to wake a lover. The lock on the bathroom door seemed about a mile away and rocking dangerously.

And he ignored her, dammit. She felt him wrap a towelling robe around her trembling shoulders.

'All right. Try to relax.'

How could she? Humiliation wasn't conducive to relaxation. 'Go away!'

'Be quiet.' His voice was firm, and Nell reckoned that begging wasn't an option. Another bout of sickness chased any further thoughts away.

'I'm sorry. I'm so sorry...' She moaned the words, wishing that she could be somewhere else. Anywhere else.

'It's okay. You're just seasick.'

'Uh. Just...?'

'You'll feel better in a minute.'

No, she wouldn't. She felt so ill that she was almost glad that Hugo was there. In between wanting him to go away and somehow forgetting that this had ever happened.

'Is that everything?'

Maybe. Nell wasn't sure, but she felt cold now, instead of burning hot. Hugo seemed to think so because he was gently guiding her to her feet.

'Come...'

'No!' At least she'd made it to the bathroom. Now she was here, she wasn't taking any chances. Hugo reached for the large, well-stocked bathroom cabinet. It seemed that in addition to condoms, which she'd found in there earlier in the evening and made use of later, the cabinet was also prepared for seasickness. Hugo took out a cardboard dish and gave it to her, collecting a bottle of ginger tablets.

He walked her through to the cabin, sitting her down on the bed. She felt a little better. Just well enough for embarrassment to take a better hold around her heart.

'The sea's a little choppier now than it was earlier.'

'Yeah? Thought it was just me.' Nell groaned as another wave of nausea took hold, but this time, she managed to quell it.

'No, it's unusually rough for this harbour. Try looking at the coastline, that might help orientate you a bit.'

Nell looked at the lights, still shining around the bay. They seemed a long way away at the moment, and enticingly still. 'Can't we…dock or something?'

'I'm afraid not. There's nowhere *to* dock.'

'Oh-h-h…!' Nowhere to run. Nowhere to hide. This was turning into a nightmare.

He supported her gently through to his cabin, saying that it was further back and so the roll of the ship would be less. If it was, Nell couldn't feel it. He let her sip water, sitting with her as she looked through the porthole, trying to tell her brain which way they were moving before her stomach reacted to it. Gave her ginger tablets to chew, but they just made her sick again.

'Drugs, Hugo…'

'Yes. I think so, too. Do you have any allergies?'

'No… I need the drugs…' Surely he wasn't going to make her go through the preliminary questions. But he did, and Nell responded automatically to his calm, gentle tone, trying to distance herself from what was happening.

He was good at this. Even the injection was accomplished with the minimum of indignity.

'That's going to work pretty quickly now.'

'Yeah… Quickly…' Thinking was suddenly like wading through treacle. All Nell could feel was Hugo's arms around her and the sudden feeling of drowsiness.

CHAPTER SIXTEEN

SHE WOKE TO half light. A slight breeze was playing through the cabin, and the sun must be shining outside the closed curtains. Nell's first thought was that she didn't feel sick any more.

Her second thought was for Hugo. He was sitting quietly in the corner of the cabin, looking the way a lover should in the morning. Freshly showered, not yet shaved, wearing a pair of shorts and a polo shirt. She wondered if he had fresh coffee somewhere and decided her stomach wasn't quite up to that.

'I'm so embarrassed.'

He didn't even pretend to shrug it off. 'Want me to show you my scar? We can feel embarrassed together.'

In an odd way, it was the nicest thing he could have said. Saying it didn't matter would have been ridiculous. Sharing the way he felt was oddly comforting.

'Your pacemaker isn't as messy as being seasick.'

He shrugged. 'You have excellent aim, which must be entirely intuitive, since you clearly weren't up to thinking about it.'

Nell smiled. 'Glad to hear it.'

'Feeling better now?'

'Yes, much. If I'd known, I'd have taken something before I came on board.'

'I should have mentioned it. But then we doctors can be

trusted to look after our own health so well.' He quirked his lips down, to give the obvious lie to the statement.

'Don't we just.'

She almost wanted him to come back to bed. Actually, she *did* want him to, but she wasn't going to ask, not after last night. Maybe that wasn't such a bad thing. It made the transition, between lovers and friends, a little easier. Something that might be laughed about even, when the sting of embarrassment had lost its bite.

We slept together, then I got seasick and he had to give me an injection. Yes, right there...

'Can you face something to eat? Toast, maybe?'

That sounded like a good idea. Something to get her back on her feet and put this behind her.

'I'd love some.' Nell was still wearing the robe that Hugo had wrapped her in last night. She pulled back the bedcovers, finding that standing up was hardly even a challenge.

'Stay here. I'll go and get a tray.' He rose, stopping to curl his arm around her shoulder to give her a hug. Hugo was clearly pretty good at this morning-after *we're still friends, aren't we?* thing. She felt him kiss the top of her head, and then he turned and walked out of the cabin.

By lunchtime, Nell felt well enough to eat some more, and then take another trip to the bridge, so that Captain Masson could demonstrate the complexities of getting back into the marina without hitting anything. She said her good-byes, and the motor launch took them back to land, where Hugo's car was waiting for them.

Something had happened last night. Something outside the obvious.

It wasn't just the amazing sex, or the look in Hugo's green eyes when he'd given himself up to her. He'd met her embarrassment with his own shame, and somehow that

had created an understanding. Acceptance in the face of
what each of them was most afraid to show.

They could be friends now. They *must* be friends, because anything less would be a tragedy. As they walked
towards the front door of his house, and Hugo turned the
key in the lock, this seemed like a new beginning. One
that would see them both succeed in the dream that Nell
had so recently begun to share. The clinic.

They left their bags in the hall for later, and walked
through to the kitchen. Hugo opened the fridge and took
a can of ginger beer out, and Nell laughed.

'No, thanks. I think I can manage without it. Would
you like a cup of tea?'

'Love one.' He was suddenly still. The man who had
moved through today with the ease of a practised diplo-
mat was suddenly unsure of himself.

'Nell...?'

'Yes?'

'Last night. I...'

She could handle this. Nell took the can from his hand,
putting it down on the countertop. He looked at it for a
moment and then his gaze moved to her face.

'I had the very best night. And then the very worst. I'm
glad you were there for the best part, and sorry you had
to be for the worst.'

'I'm not sorry...' he started.

She laid her hand lightly on his chest, and he fell silent.
'I'm very grateful you were there to look after me. That's
the advantage of sleeping with a doctor. And, like you say,
what happens at sea stays at sea. We have a clinic to build.'

He nodded. 'And you don't feel you can work with me
and sleep with me? I can understand that, if that's what
you're saying.'

At some point, she'd become a different person from

the one who had been taken in by Martin, and then bullied by him. Nell wasn't quite sure when that had happened.

'I'm think I'm still working that one out.'

'Then…are you somewhere that might allow a bit of flexibility? On the working together and sleeping together thing?'

It was as if someone had opened a door, letting sunlight into the room. All the knowledge of chemical reactions in the brain didn't make it any less a work of magic.

'What kind of flexibility?' The sudden desire to be wooed flared in her chest, making Nell's heart beat a little faster.

That smile of his was a very good opening salvo. The way he stepped a little closer, not quite touching her, made Nell's head begin to reel.

'I want to touch you again. I know I can't keep you for ever, but it doesn't make it any the less sweet that you're here now.'

Nell reached up, brushing her fingertips against his cheek. 'I want to touch you, too.'

He reached for her, pulling her close. When he kissed her, she could feel all the tension buzzing between them. Last night hadn't even begun to sate it; instead, it had only made it grow.

'Upstairs.' He whispered the word, but it still held all the promise of a command.

'Yes. Upstairs.'

It was odd. Before they'd been sleeping together, no one had doubted their devotion to one another. The papers had used the official photographs taken to celebrate their engagement and painted a rosy picture of a couple who were completely in love. But now…

Hugo was laughing on the phone with his mother as he walked her from the car to the front door. He walked into the kitchen, pulling a carton of juice from the fridge, and Nell fetched two glasses.

'Yes, I'll give her your love… Love you, too.' Hugo had seemed more openly affectionate with his mother in the last few weeks, and he'd even taken to chatting with his father on the phone.

'What was that all about?' Nell picked up her glass, taking a sip from it.

'Apparently we're cooling off.'

'Really?' Nell raised her eyebrows. She hadn't noticed anything of the sort. The last two weeks had been all heat.

'My mother was talking to a friend of hers who was at the gala we went to at the weekend. She said that I hardly looked at you all evening.'

Nell grinned. 'Perhaps we'd had an argument.'

'Perhaps. Maybe I was just looking the other way, trying not to imagine what you were wearing under that dress.'

'Oh. So you can do that, can you? Look the other way and get your imagination under control.'

'No, not really.' He took a step towards her, laying his hand on her waist. 'What are you wearing under this dress?'

'What if I said long johns?'

He laughed, taking the near-empty glass from her hand and putting it on the kitchen counter. Nell backed away from him and he followed, closing in on her.

'Long johns would be fine. Just as long as you're in them.' He wound his arms around her waist, pulling her against him, his body suddenly taut.

'Ah. What about something in stout cotton? Plenty of buttons and safety pins.'

'Wonderful. They'd take a bit more concentration to get off. I might just faint from anticipation while I do it, and then you can revive me.'

Nell laughed. Hugo loved the act of undressing her.

Made an art of it, as if he were slowly unwrapping something precious. She loved it, too. It was one of the ways he made her feel special.

'I've been wanting you all day…' Every time she touched Hugo, she wanted him. That was probably why she studiously avoided touching him in public.

'I'm glad to hear that. You want me now?' His hand slipped beneath her jacket, moving towards her breast. Nell began to tremble and she felt his lips curve into a smile against hers. 'You *do* want me. I can feel it.'

'Come and find out how much…'

Nell couldn't remember being any happier than she was now. Hugo was becoming stronger and the scar on his chest was fading. It felt as if maybe the scars in Nell's heart might be finally fading, too.

They reached their fundraising target, and celebrated it with champagne in bed. All that mattered in these early days of their heady romance was that every moment spent alone was spent in each other's arms.

They sat on the patio, eating breakfast, and Nell tore open the thick envelope, drawing out the heavily embossed paper. Hugo was watching quietly. He knew it must be a letter from the legal team he'd persuaded Nell to use in her complaint against Martin.

'What do they say?' He gave her time to read, hope kindling in his eyes when he saw her smile.

'Four other women have come forward and said that Martin made persistent and unwelcome advances towards them. Apparently one of them had the presence of mind to record him on her mobile phone.' She grinned at him. 'He used exactly the same phrases as I wrote in my complaint.'

Hugo chuckled. 'Open and shut case, then.'

'I think so. The hospital have suspended him, and there may be criminal charges in connection with one of the complaints.' She slid the letter across the table so that Hugo could read it all. 'Thank you.'

He shook his head, laughing. 'You did it all. I just… watched and admired.'

'Well, thank you for watching and admiring. You do it so well.'

They finished breakfast and drove to the hospital. Hugo had a planning meeting to attend, and Nell had decided to spend the time in the ward, helping the children's play specialist.

'It'll be great when we have more space.' The young red-headed woman grinned at Nell.

'Did Dr Bertrand tell you? We have the money now, and the work can go ahead again. There should be some progress during the next few weeks.'

'Yes, he did. We'll be able to watch it go up. I'll take pictures for you every day, so you can see what's happening.'

It was a nice thought, but Nell wondered why Louise thought she wouldn't be able to take pictures for herself. 'Thanks. I won't be here every day, so it would be good to have those.'

'You won't be here at all, will you? What about the celebrations?'

'I forgot about those,' she hedged. Maybe this was something that Hugo hadn't told her about?

'Well, once you've been, you won't forget them for next year. Montarino's royal anniversary fortnight is a bit special, there's always lots to do. I expect you'll be really busy.' Louise's voice rang with anticipation.

'Mmm. Well, yes. It would be great if you could take some photos. While I'm busy.' Nell turned her attention to the little boy who had just been wheeled into the play-room by one of the nurses, gathering up some bricks and putting them on the table in front of him.

* * *

'Montarino's royal anniversary fortnight.' Nell couldn't help keeping the sharpness from her voice. Over the course of the day, she'd made discreet enquiries about it, as well as looking it up on the Internet. Apparently the whole royal family took part, and there were concerts, exhibitions and other events over a full two weeks. Why hadn't Hugo told her about it?

A small voice at the back of her head told her why. But Nell was trying to ignore it.

'Ah. Yes.' Hugo put his car keys down on the table. 'I was going to mention that.'

His tone had a guilty ring to it. The small voice got louder.

'Okay. It's just that one of the play therapists at the hospital mentioned it. She says it's really good fun.'

'Yes, it is.'

'And that the whole royal family takes part?'

'Yes, we do. It's a tradition dating back hundreds of years. It's said there used to be a banquet that lasted two weeks, but we've skipped that bit now.'

'And it's in two weeks' time.' Nell was getting a very bad feeling now.

'Yes.' He paused, frowning. 'Nell, I think… Maybe we should give it a miss.'

'That's entirely up to you, Hugo. But shouldn't you be with your family?' Hugo seemed to be getting on so much better with his father these days. They still occasionally had their ups and downs, but Nell had encouraged Hugo to voice his affection and respect for his father. No doubt under similar pressure from his mother, Hugo's father had begun to voice similar feelings about his son.

'Well… I'll have to go to some of the events. Now that I'm back to full health, I should start taking on some of my royal duties again. I may have to stay at the palace for…a few nights. Maybe more.'

This wasn't like Hugo. He was usually so decisive. Nell knew for sure now that something was up. 'Hugo, just say it. What's going on? Don't you want me to go with you? You know I'll support you, in whatever you want to do.'

He sat down at the kitchen table, tracing his fingers across its surface. Then he seemed to come to a decision. 'I don't want you there.'

'Okay. Fine.' Nell swallowed the feeling that suddenly the world was turning in the wrong direction. It was making her feel a little sick.

'It's not that I don't want you with me. I just…' He shrugged, letting out a sigh. 'I don't want you involved with my official duties. These two weeks are always really busy and… I promised you that you'd never be just the woman on my arm. That you'd always have your own career.'

Nell didn't remember him promising her that. Maybe he'd just promised it to himself. 'I can see why you'd say that. But I don't mind. If you want me to be there, I'll happily support you. That's what we do for each other, isn't it?'

'Yes, it is. And my way of supporting you is to draw that line and stick to it. You…you've only been to one official function and that seemed…stressful for you.'

'Yes, it was stressful. You got hit with a stun gun.'

Hugo shrugged. 'I meant the bit before that. The dress and everything…'

'It was my first time, of course I was a bit stressed.' Nell frowned. 'This isn't about me, is it?'

'It's all about you, Nell. It's about my not taking you for granted, and giving you the room to have your own career.'

'It's about Anna.' His *real* fiancée. Nell felt a sudden stab of jealousy, knowing that the ring she wore was the symbol of an agreement, not of love.

'Anna's in my past. We've been finished, in every way, for a long time.'

'Yes, but what happened isn't finished. You can't let go of the idea that Montarino is your duty, and that you can't escape it. Or that your duty is incompatible with having a partner who has a career.'

'No, I can't. Because that's the truth of it, Nell. Believe me, I've tried and it doesn't work.' His voice was suddenly cold. Nell knew that she was pushing Hugo too far, into places that she'd resolved never to go with him. But if that could break them apart then maybe it should. Because it was an issue that they could only avoid for so long.

When had she started thinking about the long-term? Their engagement was one of convenience, and they'd agreed that three to six months would be enough. They'd decided to part after that.

But that was before they'd slept together. They'd promised that it would change nothing, yet it had changed everything. And suddenly Nell saw that while Hugo was kind and honourable, and Martin was neither, she would still always have to play the mistress with Hugo. His first loves were his work and his country, and he would never truly believe that there was room for her in that situation.

Nell deserved more than this. At the very minimum, she deserved his honesty. Hugo had almost deceived himself into thinking that it could work between them, but in truth he'd been careful to show her only one side of his life. Just as their engagement had sheltered her from the press, he had sheltered her from the realities of sharing her life with a prince.

Much as he wanted to, he couldn't do this to her. He couldn't take away her independence, and her career, and watch her fade and wilt in the bright light of his responsibilities.

'Nell, we agreed.' He didn't want to say it, but he had to.

'Yes, we agreed. A three-month engagement and then we go our separate ways.' As usual, she was ahead of him. The connection between them, which up till now had been a conduit for love, seemed now to be pushing them inexorably towards a parting.

'I'm fit and well now. And you're safe from the lies.' Was that really all there was to their relationship? A convenience? It had started out that way, and it seemed that it was going to end that way.

'So you'll go back to your life, and I'll go back to mine.'

'I think that's best for both of us.'

She turned away from him suddenly. As if she didn't want to even look at him any more. 'Fine. We'll do that, then.'

'Nell…' He hadn't wanted things to end like this. Maybe he should have thought about that when he'd first reached out to touch her. 'Nell, you can stay here for as long as you want. I'll go to my apartment at the palace…'

She faced him, her cheeks flushed red. Even now, if she had cried, Hugo could never have let her go, but she didn't. 'I'm not your employee, Hugo. You don't have to give me a notice period, I can leave whenever I like.'

Anger started to mount in his chest. If that was the way she wanted it. 'Fine. I'm going to the palace anyway.' He picked up his car keys and walked back outside to the car. Starting the engine, he pulled out of the driveway and onto the road.

CHAPTER SEVENTEEN

HUGO BROODED ON the matter for two weeks. Then he got on a plane and flew to London.

Nell's flat was in a nice road, with trees on each side of it. As he got out of the taxi, he noticed that her front gate needed mending, and that the brass on the front door had been recently polished. It felt as if everything had suddenly shot into sharp focus.

A young woman answered the door and stared at him blankly.

'I'm looking for Nell. Nell Maitland.'

'Oh. She's not here any more. Sorry.' The woman made to shut the front door and Hugo wondered if he should put his foot against the frame. Probably not, it might scare her.

'Please…' The door opened again, and Hugo breathed a sigh of relief. 'Do you know of any way that I might contact her?'

'No, I'm sorry. We've been here for three months and we've just signed another lease. The agent said that she was going abroad again.'

'I don't suppose you know where?'

'No. She didn't go back to…' The woman clicked her fingers, trying to recall the name.

'Montarino.'

'That's right. The agent did say that she wasn't going back there.'

Okay. That was Montarino ticked off the list. It was a start. All Hugo had to contend with now was the rest of the world.

'Would you be able to give me the name of the agent, please? I'm trying to get in contact with her.'

The woman looked him up and down, seeming to come to the conclusion that it would be okay. 'It's Green's in the High Street. You know it?'

'No, I'm sorry, I don't. Which way is that?'

'End of the road, turn left. Walk down to the very end of that road and then turn right along the High Street. You can't miss it.' The woman shrugged. 'There's a big green sign.'

'Thank you.' Hugo smiled. It seemed as if this was going to be a long journey, but this was at least the first step.

The woman smiled suddenly. 'Good luck.'

'Thank you.' He was going to need it. He had to fly back to Montarino tonight, but he had time enough to speak to the estate agent and if Nell was still in London, he might be able to see her today.

This was Nell's third job in a few weeks. Maybe this one would be a keeper.

She'd told her employment agency that she'd take any job anywhere, as long as it wasn't in London and they would guarantee absolute discretion as regards her whereabouts. They'd taken her at her word. The first job had been a week or so as a supply doctor on nights in a busy Huddersfield A & E department. The second had taken her to Manchester for a few days, and the third had brought her to Northern Germany, where she was helping an over-worked and understaffed clinic that had been set up to cater for refugees.

It might be classed as overkill, but you didn't just

walk away from Hugo. He had contacts everywhere. If he missed her one quarter as much as she missed him, he might try to get in contact. And if he did, she couldn't trust herself not to respond.

It was better not to give him that chance. Not face the dilemma of his having tried to find her, and not to feel the heartbreak if he hadn't. This way she could draw a line under their affair and find a way to start again. Let him start again, and have the life he deserved.

The clinic was hard work. Nell's German wasn't up to scratch yet, but it was improving every day, and her French and English were both useful. The families under her care tore at her heart, but it was work that was important. The director of the clinic had already asked whether she was available for another month, and she hoped that might be extended even further.

It was late, almost nine o'clock, when she finally packed up her things and grabbed her coat. Tomorrow was her one day off per week, and she might just spend that sleeping and eating, since she hadn't had a great deal of time for either in the last couple of days.

'I'll see you on Thursday.' She smiled at the receptionist, who nodded back. Pulling her coat around her against the first chill of winter, she walked outside, nodding to the security guard at the gate and making for her car, which was parked some way down the road.

He was under a lamppost, next to her car. Huddled in a thick jacket, pacing back and forth to keep warm. Hugo must have been waiting a while. Nell had one moment to escape, but then he saw her. She saw his face in the light of the lamp, and there was no running away now. He waited, suddenly still, as she walked towards him.

'Hugo.'

'Nell.' His voice was thick with emotion. It carried with it the long weeks of running and the inevitable search he must have made to find her. And suddenly that was all nothing. She wanted to fall into his arms and kiss him.

'It's cold.' There wasn't any point in asking him what he was doing here, that was obvious. And Hugo was shivering.

'Yes. They wouldn't let me into the clinic.'

'Security's pretty tight there. How long have you been waiting?'

'A couple of hours.'

Nell unlocked her car and opened the passenger door. 'Come and sit in the car.' If she switched the engine on, the heater might warm him a little.

'Would you mind coming to mine? I'm parked just around the corner.' He gave a hesitant smile. 'Heated seats.'

He'd found her. He'd come for her and had stood in the cold for hours, waiting for her. And despite everything, that unspoken connection between them was still as strong as it had ever been. This was like walking on the edge of a precipice in the darkness, but Nell couldn't stop herself. She took his arm, and Hugo started to walk.

'What's the clinic like?'

'It's tough. There are a lot of kids who are sick and have been through a lot. Adults, too. Any progress is hard won, but it's rewarding work.'

'Do you think you'll stay?'

If what he meant was would she forget about all this and come back with him to Montarino, the answer was no. Not to see their relationship crumble once more and feel that heartbreak all over again.

'Yes, I'm thinking about it.'

'Good. I'm glad you've found this.'

What did he want? To sit in the car and reminisce about old times? It didn't really matter, whatever it was, Nell knew she'd see it through to the end. He stopped beside his car and opened the passenger door. Nell got in.

He was cold, and the long wait had given all his fears the chance to settle heavily around his heart. But Hugo had found out what he wanted from life, and he wasn't going to give it up without a fight.

Nell's warmth hadn't changed. He still felt it, binding them together the way it always had. If her voice was tempered with sadness, it was the sadness that he felt in his own heart, too.

She pulled off her knitted hat, putting it in her lap with her gloves. She was staring at the steering wheel, as if that was safe middle ground. Not straight ahead, Nell was never that cold. Not at him, because he'd broken her heart. She didn't need to say it; he could see it in her eyes.

'Nell, I've thought about this a lot, and there are only four things that truly matter.'

She glanced at him, turning her gaze away quickly. 'Four?'

'Yes. That you follow your calling as a doctor. That I follow mine. That's two. The third, and most important, is that I love you.'

'But...you don't want me.'

'I've always wanted you, Nell. I sent you away because I thought I couldn't have you without you having to sacrifice number one. Now I know better.'

She turned suddenly, wide-eyed. 'And the fourth?'

'That's up to you. If *you* love *me*, then we can work everything else out.'

Her lip began to quiver. If she cried now he wouldn't be able to stop his own tears. Maybe that was just yet another proof of the connection that he felt with Nell.

'What about Montarino?'

Hope thumped almost painfully in his chest, and he ignored it. It was just his heart beating, and that was proof that he could live long enough to show Nell how much he loved her.

'There are people who will oversee the building of the clinic, just as well as I can. The royal calendar can do without me from time to time, my parents have it all pretty well tied down. Montarino doesn't need me, it was me who needed Montarino. I needed something to dedicate myself to.'

'And you don't now?' She frowned, shaking her head. 'Hugo, you love the place.'

'Yes, I love it. It'll always be my home. But you're the one and only love of my life, Nell. You're a lot more important to me.'

Her gaze searched his face. Then one tear dropped from her eye, tumbling down her cheek. 'You're the one and only love of my life, too.'

He reached for her, wishing that they were somewhere less cramped so he could hold her properly. But it didn't matter. Hugo knew what really mattered now, and that was being able to look into her eyes. Wipe away her tears and brush a kiss onto her lips.

'Where are you staying?' Finally she broke the warm silence that curled around them like a blanket.

'At the Grand.'

'That's right across town!'

'I booked it from the lamppost. There wasn't a great deal of choice.'

Nell chuckled. 'Okay, so we can drive across town and have room service, or it's ten minutes to mine. Fifteen if we stop for pizza on the way.'

'Pizza sounds great.'

Crown Prince Hugo Phillipe DeLeon, only son of the King of Montarino, had to carry the pizza up three flights of stairs because the lift was broken. He looked around her flat, which didn't take long, because there were only two rooms and a bathroom, and pronounced it delightful. He kept his coat on while the heating took the edge off the chill in the sitting room.

They ate pizza and drank coffee, and her small flat became the centre of the world. The one place where they could both be happy, because it was the place they were together. Curled up on the sofa together, talking about plans and dreams, futures and possibilities.

'That's what we'll do, then?' The sun was rising but Nell didn't feel tired any more.

'You're sure that's what you want?' Hugo leaned over, kissing her.

'I'm sure. You're sure you really *can* take a holiday for the next month? So that I won't let the clinic here down?'

'Positive. I'll be waiting here for you every evening with a smile on my face and a tasty meal in the oven.'

Nell snorted with laughter. 'You will not. If you're staying here, you can earn your keep. I'm sure the clinic will take you on, they could do with more doctors. And being a prince has its advantages.'

'They don't have to pay me?'

'Yeah, they don't really have the funds for that. You'll spread a little happiness, though.'

'That sounds great. Can't wait to start.' Hugo got to his feet, stretching his limbs, and walked over to the window, looking out at the glow on the horizon. 'Come with me.'

'Where are we going?'

'See that little park down there? It looks a nice place for an early morning stroll. We can watch the sunrise.'

They pulled on their coats, tiptoeing down the stairs so as not to wake any of the neighbours. Across the street and through the park gates, into a cold, fresh morning. Hugo seemed to know exactly where he wanted to go, and Nell followed him over to a small playground, sitting next to him on the swings.

He grinned, feeling in his coat pocket. Then he opened

a box, holding it out for her to see the ring inside, flashing bright in the new day. 'Nell, this is a symbol of love between the two of us. That you'll love me, and I'll love you. That we can make happen the things we both want.'

He'd said almost those same words before. This time it was real. Nell began to tremble with excitement, as he fell onto one knee in front of her. 'Will you marry me, Nell?'

'Yes, Hugo.' She leaned forward, kissing him. Holding on to him tightly, in case this was just a beautiful dream.

'This isn't a royal jewel. If you'd prefer one of those, there are plenty to choose from…'

'No. No, Hugo, this is much better. I want this one, please.' It wasn't some anonymous jewel. Hugo had chosen this just for her. It was exquisite, a gold band with square cut diamonds set all the way around it. Clearly expensive, but not so bulky that it would tear a pair of surgical gloves.

'You don't need to take this one off when you're at work.' Hugo had obviously been thinking exactly the same as she was.

'Hugo, thank you for coming for me. Thank you for believing in me. I'll never take it off.' Nell could feel tears streaming down her cheeks. He pulled at her glove, tugging it off, and she held out her hand.

'I'll be taking it off on our wedding day. Just for long enough to slip your wedding ring on.' He kissed her, sliding the ring onto her finger.

'Come home with me, Hugo. I have a three-quarter-sized bed, and I want to see how well you fit into it.'

'I'll fit. Particularly if I have you in my arms. Are you tired?'

'What? No, I'm not tired. Are you?'

'Not even slightly.' He got to his feet, wrapping his arm around her shoulders. Then Nell walked her prince back up to the tiny flat that now contained every dream she'd ever had.

EPILOGUE

THEY'D STAYED ON at the clinic in Germany for two months, working for nothing so that other doctors could be recruited and paid. Hugo bade the little flat goodbye with more regret than he'd ever left anywhere before. It held the best memories of his life.

But there was more to come. Nell was a quiet force to be reckoned with, planning a wedding and a reception that didn't follow any royal protocol that Hugo had ever heard of. The idea was received with hardly a murmur from his father, and warm approval from his mother.

Everything went off without a hitch. Nell's father and his had become friends over a shared interest in gardening, and Hugo's mother had finally managed to persuade Nell's mother that her outfit was perfect for the occasion. They were married in the presence of close family and friends in a small private ceremony. Nell looked more beautiful than he could ever have imagined, wearing a knee-length fitted dress in cream silk, her only concession to royal splendour being a small diamond tiara, which held a shoulder-length veil in place.

There was nothing but love. When he recited his vows, and she said hers. When he slipped the ring onto her finger. But the moment that made Hugo proudest was the one when his new bride took his arm and he walked into the children's cardiac unit at the hospital. She sat with each of the children, letting them hold her bouquet and even taking off the tiara so that the little girls could try it on.

Then there was cake in the children's playroom, which for some reason that Hugo couldn't fathom had candles on it. It turned out that one of the children had a birthday today, and Nell duly helped her to blow out the candles, to cheers and clapping from the parents. The nurses supervised the cutting and distribution of the cake, while Nell managed to retrieve the tiara, finding a handkerchief to wipe the sticky finger marks off it.

'Oh, dear.' She held it up to the light, twisting it back and forth. 'It's got icing on it.'

'Probably the best use it's ever been put to.' Hugo grinned, sitting down next to her on one of the plastic chairs that lined the ward. 'I dare say my mother will know the best way to clean it.'

'I can't give it back to your mother like this. She's already been so good about delaying the start of the reception so that we could come here first.'

'I thought it was rather a good idea. Gives everyone a chance to put their feet up and loosen their ties.'

'Like you've loosened yours?' Nell gave him a mischievous look. 'What *will* people say?'

'They'll say I've married the most beautiful woman in the world. The most dedicated doctor and…' Hugo brushed a crushed petal from her dress '…the best person I know.'

'And I've married the most handsome prince in the world. Actually, I should widen the scope a bit. The most handsome *doctor* in the world.'

'I like that a lot better.' Hugo kissed her hand, and heard a camera shutter click. He turned and smiled, his arm around his new wife. A picture for the hospital scrapbook.

'I'm so proud of you, Hugo. Last week, a man told me how much your speech about having a pacemaker had meant to his wife. She said that if it was good enough for you, then it was good enough for her.'

'And I'm proud of you, too. Your project is going to make a big difference to a lot of people.'

He and Nell had decided that they would work together, but each concentrate on different special projects. Nell had already formed a partnership between the hospital in Montarino and the London hospital where she'd worked, to create a joint initiative to promote research and care for elderly patients with heart disease.

'I hope so. It's early days yet.'

'We have plenty of time. All our lives.'

Nell smiled at him. 'I'm so happy, Hugo. You're my one true love.'

'And you are mine.' Hugo kissed his wife, and a cheer went up around the room.

'Do it again!' a child's voice piped up from somewhere, and everyone laughed.

There was nothing else he could do but kiss Nell again.

* * * * *

COMING SOON!

We really hope you enjoyed reading this book. If you're looking for more romance, be sure to head to the shops when new books are available on

Thursday
26th July

MILLS & BOON

Coming next month

THE SHY NURSE'S REBEL DOC
Alison Roberts

She had to catch his gaze again and she knew that her curiosity would be evident. What surprised her was seeing a reflection of that curiosity in *his* gaze.

'It was a one-off for more than the fact that neither of us do relationships,' she said. 'We work together. It would be unprofessional.'

Blake snorted softly. 'It's pretty unprofessional to be thinking about it all the time.'

Again, Sam seemed to see her own thoughts reflected in those dark eyes. He had been finding this as difficult as she had? Wow…

Could Blake hear how hard her heart was thumping right now? 'Um… maybe we just need to get it out of our system, then.'

His voice was a low, sexy rumble. 'Are you suggesting what I think you're suggesting? Another… one-off?'

'Or a two-off. A three-off, if that's what it takes.' She took a deep breath and then held his gaze steadily as she gathered her words. Yes, she did want a real relationship that was going somewhere but it had to be with the right person and that person wasn't going to be Blake Cooper because she could sense that his demons were even bigger than hers.

But, oh… that didn't stop the *wanting*, did it? The lure of the bad boy…

'We both walk alone, Blake,' she said quietly, 'for whatever reason – and at some point we'll know it's enough.

Maybe we just need to agree that when one of us reaches that point, the other walks away too. No regrets. No looking back.'

Somehow, she had moved closer to Blake as she'd been speaking, without realising it. Her head was tilted up so that she could hold his gaze and he was looking down.

Leaning down… as if he couldn't resist the urge to kiss her.

Then he straightened suddenly and Sam could feel the distance increasing between them with a wave of disappointment. Despair, almost…?

But he was smiling. That crooked, irresistibly charming smile of a man who knew exactly what he wanted and was quite confident he was going to get it.

'What are you doing tonight, Sam?'

Her mouth felt dry. 'Nothing important.'

'Give me your address and I'll come and get you. You up for a bike ride?'

Sam could almost hear her mother shrieking in horror at the thought but her rebellious streak wasn't about to be quashed. She might only get one more night with this man so why not add an extra thrill to it?

She could feel her smile stretching into a grin. 'Bring it on.'

Continue reading
THE SHY NURSE'S REBEL DOC
Alison Roberts

Available next month
www.millsandboon.co.uk

LET'S TALK
Romance

For exclusive extracts, competitions
and special offers, find us online:

f facebook.com/millsandboon

📷 @millsandboonuk

🐦 @millsandboon

Or get in touch on 0844 844 1351*

For all the latest titles coming soon, visit
millsandboon.co.uk/nextmonth